BY CHARLES BUKOWSKI
AVAILABLE FROM ECCO

The Days Run Away Like Wild Horses Over the Hills (1969)

Post Office (1971)

Mockingbird Wish Me Luck (1972)

South of No North (1973)

Burning in Water, Drowning in Flame: Selected Poems 1955–1973 (1974)

Factotum (1975)

Love Is a Dog from Hell: Poems 1974–1977 (1977)

Women (1978)

Play the Piano Drunk /Like a Percussion Instrument/
    Until the Fingers Begin to Bleed a Bit (1979)

Shakespeare Never Did This (1979)

Dangling in the Tournefortia (1981)

Ham on Rye (1982)

Bring Me Your Love (1983)

Hot Water Music (1983)

There's No Business (1984)

War All the Time: Poems 1981–1984 (1984)

You Get So Alone at Times That It Just Makes Sense (1986)

The Movie: "Barfly" (1987)

The Roominghouse Madrigals: Early Selected Poems 1946–1966 (1988)

Hollywood (1989)

Septuagenarian Stew: Stories & Poems (1990)

The Last Night of the Earth Poems (1992)

Screams from the Balcony: Selected Letters 1960–1970 (1993)

Pulp (1994)

Living on Luck: Selected Letters 1960s–1970s (Volume 2) (1995)

Betting on the Muse: Poems & Stories (1996)

Bone Palace Ballet: New Poems (1997)

The Captain Is Out to Lunch and the Sailors Have Taken Over the Ship (1998)

Reach for the Sun: Selected Letters 1978–1994 (Volume 3) (1999)

What Matters Most Is How Well You Walk Through the Fire: New Poems (1999)

Open All Night: New Poems (2000)

The Night Torn Mad with Footsteps: New Poems (2001)

Beerspit Night and Cursing: The Correspondence of Charles Bukowski & Sheri Martinelli
    1960–1967 (2001)

CHARLES BUKOWSKI

YOU GET SO ALONE AT TIMES THAT IT JUST MAKES SENSE

ecco
An Imprint of HarperCollinsPublishers

Previously published by Black Sparrow Press

HarperCollins books may be purchased for educational, business, or sales promotional use. For information, please e-mail the Special Markets Department at SPsales@harpercollins.com.

First Ecco edition published in 2002

The Library of Congress has catalogued a previous editions as follows:

Bukowski, Charles.
  You get so alone at times that it just makes sense.

  I. Title.
  PS3552.U4Y6   1986   813'.54   86-13662
  ISBN 0-87685-684-9
  ISBN 0-87685-683-0 (pbk.)

  22 23 24 LSC 50 49 48 47 46 45 44

for Jeff Copland

Contents

**you get so alone at times
that it just makes sense**

1813–1883

listening to Wagner
as outside in the dark the wind blows a cold rain the
trees wave and shake lights go
off and on the walls creak and the cats run under the
bed . . .

Wagner battles the agonies, he's emotional but
solid, he's the supreme fighter, a giant in a world of
pygmies, he takes it straight on through, he breaks
barriers
an
astonishing FORCE of sound as

everything here shakes
shivers
bends
blasts
in fierce gamble

yes, Wagner and the storm intermix with the wine as
nights like this run up my wrists and up into my head and
back down into the
gut

some men never
die
and some men never
live

but we're all alive
tonight.

red Mercedes

naturally, we are all caught in
downmoods, it's a matter of
chemical imbalance
and an existence
which, at times,
seems to forbid
any real chance at
happiness.

I was in a downmood
when this rich pig
along with his blank
inamorata
in this red Mercedes
cut
in front of me
at racetrack parking.

it clicked inside of me
in a flash:
I'm going to pull that fucker
out of his car and
kick his
ass!

I followed him
into Valet parking
parked behind him
and jumped from my
car
ran up to his
door
and yanked at

it.
it was
locked.
the
windows were
up.

I rapped on the window
on his
side:
"open up! I'm gonna
bust your
ass!"

he just sat there
looking straight
ahead.
his woman did
likewise.
they wouldn't look
at me.

he was 30 years
younger
but I knew I could
take him
he was soft and
pampered.

I beat on the window
with my
fist:
"come on out, shithead,
or I'm going to start
breaking
glass!"

he gave a small nod
to his
woman.

I saw her reach
into the glove
compartment
open it
and slip him the
.32

I saw him hold it
down low
and snap off the
safety.

I walked off
toward the
clubhouse, it looked
like a damned good
card
that
day.

all I had to do
was
be there.

retired

pork chops, said my father, I love
pork chops!

and I watched him slide the grease
into his mouth.

pancakes, he said, pancakes with
syrup, butter and bacon!

I watched his lips heavy wetted with
all that.

coffee, he said, I like coffee so hot
it burns my throat!

sometimes it was too hot and he spit it
out across the table.

mashed potatoes and gravy, he said, I
love mashed potatoes and gravy!

he jowled that in, his cheeks puffed as
if he had the mumps.

chili and beans, he said, I love chili and
beans!

and he gulped it down and farted for hours
loudly, grinning after each fart.

strawberry shortcake, he said, with vanilla
ice cream, that's the way to end a meal!

he always talked about retirement, about
what he was going to do when he
retired.
when he wasn't talking about food he talked
on and on about
retirement.

he never made it to retirement, he died one day while
standing at the sink
filling a glass of water.
he straightened like he'd been
shot.
the glass fell from his hand
and he dropped backwards
landing flat
his necktie slipping to the
left.

afterwards
people said they couldn't believe
it.
he looked
great.
distinguished white
sideburns, pack of smokes in his
shirt pocket, always cracking
jokes, maybe a little
loud and maybe with a bit of bad
temper
but all in all
a seemingly sound
individual

never missing a day
of work.

working it out

in this steamy a.m. Hades claps its Herpes hands and
a woman sings through my radio, her voice comes clambering
through the smoke, and the wine fumes . . .

it's a lonely time, she sings, and you're not
mine and it makes me feel so bad,
this thing of being me . . .

I can hear cars on the freeway, it's like a distant sea
sludged with people
while over my other shoulder, far over on 7th street
near Western
is the hospital, that house of agony —
sheets and bedpans and arms and heads and
expirations;
everything is so sweetly awful, so continuously and
sweetly awful: the art of consummation: life eating
life . . .
once in a dream I saw a snake swallowing its own
tail, it swallowed and swallowed until
it got halfway round, and there it stopped and
there it stayed, it was stuffed with its own
self. some fix, that.
we only have ourselves to go on, and it's
enough . . .

I go downstairs for another bottle, switch on the
cable and there's Greg Peck pretending he's
F. Scott and he's very excited and he's reading his
manuscript to his lady.
I turn the set
off.

what kind of writer is that? reading his pages to
a lady? this is a violation . . .

I return upstairs and my two cats follow me, they are
fine fellows, we have no discontent, we have no
arguments, we listen to the same music, never vote for a
president.
one of my cats, the big one, leaps on the back
of my chair, rubs against my shoulders and
neck.

"no good," I tell him, "I'm not going
to read you this
poem."

he leaps to the floor and walks out to the
balcony and his buddy
follows.

they sit and watch the night; we've got the
power of sanity here.

these early a.m. mornings when almost everybody
is asleep, small night bugs, winged things
enter, and circle and whirl.
the machine hums its electric hum, and having
opened and tasted the new bottle I type the next
line. you
can read it to your lady and she'll probably tell you
it's nonsense. she'll be
reading *Tender Is the
Night.*

beasts bounding through time—

Van Gogh writing his brother for paints
Hemingway testing his shotgun
Celine going broke as a doctor of medicine
the impossibility of being human
Villon expelled from Paris for being a thief
Faulkner drunk in the gutters of his town
the impossibility of being human
Burroughs killing his wife with a gun
Mailer stabbing his
the impossibility of being human
Maupassant going mad in a rowboat
Dostoevsky lined up against a wall to be shot
Crane off the back of a boat into the propeller
the impossibility
Sylvia with her head in the oven like a baked potato
Harry Crosby leaping into that Black Sun
Lorca murdered in the road by the Spanish troops
the impossibility
Artaud sitting on a madhouse bench
Chatterton drinking rat poison
Shakespeare a plagiarist
Beethoven with a horn stuck into his head against deafness
the impossibility the impossibility
Nietzsche gone totally mad
the impossibility of being human
all too human
this breathing
in and out
out and in
these punks
these cowards
these champions
these mad dogs of glory

moving this little bit of light toward
us
impossibly.

trashcan lives

the wind blows hard tonight
and it's a cold wind
and I think about
the boys on the row.
I hope some of them have a bottle
of red.

it's when you're on the row
that you notice that
everything
is owned
and that there are locks on
everything.
this is the way a democracy
works:
you get what you can,
try to keep that
and add to it
if possible.

this is the way a dictatorship
works too
only they either enslave or
destroy their
derelicts.

we just forget
ours.

in either case
it's a hard
cold
wind.

the lost generation

have been reading a book about a rich literary lady
of the twenties and her husband who
drank, ate and partied their way through
Europe
meeting Pound, Picasso, A. Huxley, Lawrence, Joyce,
F. Scott, Hemingway, many
others;
the famous were like precious toys to
them,
and the way it reads
the famous allowed themselves to become
precious toys.
all through the book
I waited for just *one* of the famous
to tell this rich literary lady and her
rich literary husband to
get off and out
but, apparently, none of them ever
did.
Instead they were photographed with the lady
and her husband
at various seasides
looking intelligent
as if all this was part of the act
of Art.
perhaps because the wife and husband
fronted a lush press that
had something to do
with it.
and they were all photographed together
at parties
or outside of Sylvia Beach's bookshop.
it's true that many of them were

great and/or original artists,
but it all seems such a snobby precious
affair,
and the husband finally committed his
threatened suicide
and the lady published one of my first
short stories in the
40's and is now
dead, yet
I can't forgive either of them
for their rich dumb lives
and I can't forgive their precious toys
either
for being
that.

no help for that

there is a place in the heart that
will never be filled

a space

and even during the
best moments
and
the greatest
times

we will know it

we will know it
more than
ever

there is a place in the heart that
will never be filled

and

we will wait
and
wait

in that
space.

my non-ambitious ambition

my father had little sayings which he mostly shared
during dinner sessions; food made him think of
survival:
"succeed or suck eggs . . ."
"the early bird gets the worm . . ."
"early to bed and early to rise makes a man (etc.) . . ."
"anybody who wants to can make it in America . . ."
"God takes care of those who (etc.) . . ."

I had no particular idea who he was talking
to, and personally I thought him a
crazed and stupid brute
but my mother *always* interspersed these
sessions with: "Henry, *listen* to your
father."

at that age I didn't have any other
choice
but as the food went down with the
sayings
the appetite and the digestion went
along with them.

it seemed to me that I had never met
another person on earth
as discouraging to my happiness
as my father.

and it appeared that I had
the same effect upon
him.

"You are a *bum*," he told me, "and you'll
always be a *bum*!"

and I thought, if being a bum is to be the
opposite of what this son-of-a-bitch
is, then that's what I'm going to
be.

and it's too bad he's been dead
so long
for now he can't see
how beautifully I've succeeded
at
that.

education

at that small inkwell desk
I had trouble with the words
"sing" and "sign."
I don't know why
but
"sing" and "sign":
it bothered
me.

the others went on and learned
new things
but I just sat there
thinking about
"sing" and "sign."
there was something there
I couldn't
overcome.

what it gave me was a
bellyache as
I looked at the backs of all those
heads.

the lady teacher had a
very fierce face
it ran sharply to a
point
and was heavy with white
powder.

one afternoon
she asked my mother to come
see her

and I sat with them
in the classroom
as they
talked.

"he's not learning
anything," the teacher
told my
mother.

"please give him a
chance, Mrs. Sims!"

"he's not *trying,* Mrs.
Chinaski!"

my mother began to
cry.

Mrs. Sims sat there
and watched
her.

it went on for some
minutes.

then Mrs. Sims said,
"well, we'll see what we
can do . . ."

then I was walking with
my mother
we were walking in
front of the school,
there was much green grass

and then the
sidewalk.

"oh, Henry," my mother said,
"your father is so disappointed in
you, I don't know what we are
going to do!"

father, my mind said,
father and father and
father.

words like that.

I decided not to learn anything
in that
school.

my mother walked along
beside me.
she wasn't anything at
all.
and I had a bellyache
and even the trees we walked
under
seemed less than
trees
and more like everything
else.

downtown L.A.

throwing your shoe at 3 a.m. and smashing the window, then
    sticking
your head through the shards of glass and laughing as the
    phone rings
with authoritative threats as you curse back through the
    receiver, slam
it down as the woman screeches: "WHAT THE FUCK YA
    DOIN', YA ASSHOLE!"

you smirk, look at her (what's this?), you're cut somewhere,
    love it, the
dripping of red onto your dirty torn undershirt, the whiskey
    roaring
through your invincibility: you're young, you're big, and the
    world
stinks from centuries of Humanity while

you're on course
and there's something left to drink—
it's good, it's a dramatic farce and you can handle it with
verve, style, grace and elite
mysticism.

another hotel drunk—thank god for hotels and whiskey and
    ladies of the
street!

you turn to her: "you chippy hunk of shit, don't bad mouth
    me! I'm
the toughest guy in town, you don't know who the hell you're
    in this room
with!"

she just looks, half-believing . . . a cigarette dangling, she's half-
insane, looking for an out; she's hard, she's scared, she's been
fooled, taken, abused, used, over-
used . . .

but, under all that, to me she's the *flower,* I see her as she was
before she was ruined by the lies: theirs and
hers.

to me, she's new again as I am new: we have a chance
together.

I walk over and fill her drink: "you got class, doll, you're not
    like the
others . . ."

she likes that and I like it too because to make a thing true all
    you've
got to do is believe.

I sit across from her as she tells me about her life, I give her
    refills,
light her cigarettes, I listen and the City of the Angels
listens: she's had a hard row.

I get sentimental and decide not to fuck her: one more man for
    her
won't help and one more woman for me won't
matter—besides, she doesn't look that
good.

actually, her life is boring and rather common but most are—
    mine is too
except when lifted by
whiskey

she gets into a crying-jag, she's cute, really, and pitiful, all she
     wants
is what she always wanted, only it's getting further and further
away.

then she stops crying, we just drink and smoke, it's
peaceful—I won't bother her that
night . . .

I have trouble trying to yank the pull-down bed from the wall,
     she
comes up to help, we pull together—suddenly, it
     releases—flings
itelf upon us, a hard death-like mindless object, it knocks us
     upon
our asses beneath it as
first in fear we scream
then begin laughing, laughing like
crazy.

she gets the bathroom first, then I use it, then we stretch out
     and
sleep.

I am awakened in the early morning . . . she is down at my
     center, she has
me in her mouth and is working furiously.

"it's all right," I say, "you don't have to do
that."

she continues, finishes . . .

in the morning we pass the desk clerk, he has on thick-rimmed
    dark glasses,
seems to sit in the shade of some tarantula dream: he was there
    when we
entered, he is there now: some eternal darkness, we are almost
    to the door
when he says:
"don't come back."

we walk 2 blocks up, turn left, walk one block, then one block
    south, enter
Willie's at the middle of the
block, place ourselves at bar
center.

we order beer for starters, we sit there as she searches her purse
    for
cigarettes, then I get up, move toward the juke box, put a coin
within, come back, sit down, she lifts her glass, "the first one's
    best,"
and I lift my drink, "and the last . . ."

outside, the traffic runs up and down, down and
up,
going
nowhere.

another casualty

cat got run over
now silver screw holding together a broken
femur
right leg
bound in bright red
bandage

got cat home from vet's
took my eye off
him for
a moment

he ran across floor
dragging his red
leg
chasing the female
cat

worst thing the
fucker could
do

he's in the penalty
box
now
sweating it
out

he's just like the
rest of
us

he has these large

yellow eyes
staring

only wanting to
live the
good
life.

driving test

drivers
in defense and anger
often give the
finger
to those
who become involved in their
driving problems.

I am aware what the
signal of the finger
implies
yet when it is directed
at me
sometimes
I can't help laughing at
the florid
twisted
faces
and
the gesture.

yet today
I found myself
giving the finger
to some guy
who pulled directly
into my lane
without waiting
from a supermarket
exit.

I shook the finger at
him.

he saw it
and I drove along right on his
rear
bumper.

it was my first
time.

I was a member of the
club
and I felt like a
fucking
fool.

that's why funerals are so sad

he's got all the tools but he's lazy, has no
fire, the ladies drain his senses, his
emotions, he just wants to drive his
flashy car
he gets a wax job once a month
throws away his shoes when they get
scuffed
but
he's got the best right hand in the
business
and his left hook can cave in a man's ribs
if I can get him to do it
but
he has no god damned imagination
he's in the top ten
but the music is missing.
he makes the money
but it's all going to get away from
him.
some day he's not going to be able to do
even the little
he's doing now.
his idea of victory is to pull down as
many women's panties as he
can.
he's
champ at that.
and when you see me screaming at him
in his corner between
rounds
I'm trying to awaken him to the fact that
the TIME is
NOW.

he just grins at me:
"hell, *you* fight him, he's a
bitch . . ."

you have no idea, cousin, how many
men
can do it
but
won't.

cornered

well, they said it would come to
this: old. talent gone. fumbling for
the word

hearing the dark
footsteps, I turn
look behind me . . .

not yet, old dog . . .
soon enough.

now
they sit talking about
me: "yes, it's happened, he's
finished . . . it's
sad . . ."

"he never had a great deal, did
he?"

"well, no, but now . . ."

now
they are celebrating my demise
in taverns I no longer
frequent.

now
I drink alone
at this malfunctioning
machine

as the shadows assume
shapes
I fight the slow
retreat

now
my once-promise
dwindling
dwindling

now
lighting new cigarettes
pouring more
drinks

it has been a beautiful
fight

still
is.

bumming with Jane

there wasn't a stove
and we put cans of beans
in hot water in the sink
to heat them
up
and we read the Sunday papers
on Monday
after digging them out of the
trash cans
but somehow we managed
money for wine
and the
rent
and the money came off
the streets
out of hock shops
out of nowhere
and all that mattered
was the next
bottle
and we drank and sang
and
fought
were in and out
of drunk
tanks
car crashes
hospitals
we barricaded ourselves
against the
police
and the other roomers
hated

us
and the desk clerk
of the hotel
feared
us
and it went on
and
on
and it was one of the
most wonderful times
of my
life.

darkness

darkness falls upon Humanity
and faces become terrible
things
that wanted more than there
was.

all our days are marked with
unexpected
affronts — some
disastrous, others
less so
but the process is
wearing and
continuous.
attrition rules.
most give
way
leaving
empty spaces
where people should
be.

our progenitors, our
educational systems, the
land, the media, the
way
have
deluded and misled the
masses: they have been
defeated
by the aridity of
the *actual*
dream.

they were
unaware that
achievement or victory or
luck or
whatever the hell you
want to call
it
must have
its defeats.

it's only the re-gathering and
going on
which lends substance
to whatever magic
might possibly
evolve.

and now
as we ready to self-destruct
there is very little left to
kill

which makes the tragedy
less and more
much much
more.

termites of the page

the problem that I've found with
most poets that I have known is that
they've never had an 8 hour job
and there is nothing
that will put a person
more in touch
with the realities
than
an 8 hour job.

most of these poets
that I have known
have
seemingly existed on
air alone
but
it hasn't been truly
so:
behind them has been
a family member
usually a wife or mother
supporting these
souls
and
so it's no wonder
they have written so
poorly:
they have been protected
against the actualities
from the
beginning
and they
understand nothing

but the ends of their
fingernails
and
their delicate
hairlines
and
their lymph
nodes.

their words are
unlived, unfurnished, un-
true, and worse — so
fashionably
dull.

soft and safe
they gather together to
plot, hate,
gossip, most of these
American poets
pushing and hustling their
talents
playing at
greatness.

poet (?):
that word needs re-
defining.

when I hear that
word
I get a rising in the
gut
as if I were about to
puke.

let them have the
stage
so long
as I need not be
in the
audience.

a good time

now look, she said, stretched out on the bed, I don't want
    anything
personal, let's just do it, I don't want to get involved, got
it?

she kicked off her high-heeled shoes . . .

sure, he said, standing there, let's just pretend that we've
already done it, there's nothing less involved than that, is
there?

what the hell do you mean? she asked.

I mean, he said, I'd rather drink
anyhow.

and he poured himself one.

it was a lousy night in Vegas and he walked to the window
    and
looked out at the dumb lights.

you a fag? she asked, you a god damned
fag?

no, he said.

you don't have to get shitty, she said, just because you lost at
the tables—we drove all the way here to have a good time and
now look at you: sucking at that booze, you coulda done that
    in
L.A.!

right, he said, one thing I do like to get involved with is the
fucking bottle.

I want you to take me home, she said.

my pleasure, he said, let's
go.

it was one of those times where nothing was lost because
      nothing
had ever been found and as she got dressed it was sad for
him
not because of him and the lady but because of all the millions
like him and the lady
as the lights blinked out there, everything so effort-
lessly false.

she was ready, fast: let's get the hell out of here, she
said.

right, he said, and they walked out the door together.

the still trapeze

Saroyan told his wife, "I've got to
gamble in order to
write." she told him to
go ahead.

he lost $350,000.00
mostly at the racetrack
but still couldn't write *or*
pay his taxes.

he ran from the govt. and exiled himself
in Paris.

he later came back, sweated it
out
in hock up to his
ass —
royalties dropping
off.

he still couldn't write or
what he wrote didn't
work
because that tremendous
brave optimism
that buoyed everybody up
so well
during the depression
just turned to
sugar water
during
good times.

he died
a dwindling legend
with a huge handlebar
mustache
just like his father
used to have
in the old Fresno
Armenian way
in a world that
could no longer
use
William.

January

here
you see this
hand

here you see this
sky
this
bridge

hear this
sound

the agony of the
elephant

the nightmare of the
midget

while
caged parrots
sit in a
flourish of
color

while pieces of
people
fall over the
edge
like pebbles
like
rocks

madhouses screaming in
pain

as the royalty of the
world is
photographed
say
on horseback
or
say
watching a procession
in their
honor

as
the junkies junk
as the alkies drink
as the whores whore
as the killers kill

the albatross blinks its
eyes

the weather stays
mostly
the same.

sunny side down

NOTHING. sitting in a cafe having breakfast. NOTHING. the
    waitress,
and the people eating. the traffic runs by. doesn't matter what
Napoleon did, what Plato said. Turgenev could have been a fly.
    we are worn-
down, hope stamped out. we reach for coffee cups like the
    robots about
to replace us. courage at Salerno, bloodbaths on the Eastern
    front didn't
matter. we know that we are beaten. NOTHING. now it's just
    a matter of
continuing
            anyhow —
chew the food and read the paper. we
read about ourselves. the news is
bad. something about
NOTHING.
Joe Louis long dead as the medfly invades Beverly Hills.
well, at least we can sit and
eat. it's been some rough
trip. it could be
worse. it could be worse than
NOTHING.

let's get more coffee from the
waitress.
that *bitch*! she knows we are trying to get her
attention.
she just stands there doing
NOTHING.
it doesn't matter if Prince Charles falls off his horse
or that the hummingbird is so seldom
seen

or that we are too senseless to go
insane.

coffee. give us more of that NOTHING
coffee.

the man in the brown suit

fuck, he was small
maybe 5-3,
135 pounds,
I didn't like
him,
he sat there at his desk
at the
bank
and as I waited in line
he seemed to have a way
of glancing at
me
and I stared
back,
I don't know what
it was
that caused the
animosity.
he had this little mustache
that drooped
at the ends,
he was in his mid-forties
and like most people who worked
in banks
he had a non-committal
yet self-important
personality.

one day I almost went
over the railing
to ask him
what the hell

was he looking
at?

today I went in
and stood in line
and saw him leave his
desk.
one of the lady tellers was
having a problem
with a man
at her
window
and the man
in the brown suit
began to hold
counsel with both of
them.
suddenly
the man in the brown suit
vaulted the
railing
got behind the other
man
wrapped his arms
about him
then dragged him along
to a latch
entrance
along the railing
reached over
unhooked the latch
while still managing to
hold the
man.

then he dragged him
in there
latched the
gate
and while holding the
man
he told one of the
girls,
"Phone the
police."

the man he was holding was
about 20, black, a good 6-2,
maybe 190 pounds,
and I thought, hey,
break loose, man, jail is a
long time.

but he just stood
there
being
held.

I left before the
police
arrived.

the next time
I went to the bank
the man in the brown suit
was behind his
desk.
and when he glanced at
me
I smiled just a
little.

a magician, gone . . .

they go one by one and as they do it gets closer
to me and
I don't mind that so much, it's
just that I can't be practical about the
mathematics that take others
to the vanishing point.

last Saturday
one of racing's greatest harness drivers
died—little Joe O'Brien.
I had seen him win many a
race. he
had a peculiar rocking motion
he flicked the reins
and rocked his body back and
forth. he
applied this motion
during the stretch run and
it was quite dramatic and
effective . . .

he was so small that he couldn't
lay the whip on as hard as the
others
so
he rocked and rocked
in the sulky
and the horse felt the lightning
of his excitement
that rhythmic crazy rocking was
transferred from man to
beast . . .
the whole thing had the feel of a

crapshooter calling to the
gods, and the gods
so often answered . . .

I saw Joe O'Brien win
endless photo finishes
many by a
nose.
he'd take a horse
another driver couldn't get a
run out of
and Joe would put his touch
to it
and the animal would
most often respond with
a flurry of wild energy.

Joe O'Brien was the finest harness driver
I had ever seen
and I'd seen many over the
decades.
nobody could nurse and cajole
a trotter or a pacer
like little Joe
nobody could make the magic work
like Joe.

they go one by one
presidents
garbage men
killers
actors
pickpockets
boxers
hit men
ballet dancers

fishermen
doctors
fry cooks
like
that

but Joe O'Brien
it's going to be hard
hard
to find a replacement for
little Joe

and
at the ceremony
held for him
at the track tonight
(Los Alamitos 10-1-84)
as the drivers gathered in a
circle
in their silks
at the finish line
I had to turn my back
to the crowd
and climb the upper grandstand
steps
to the wall
so the people wouldn't
see me
cry.

well, that's just the way it is . . .

sometimes when everything seems at
its worst
when all conspires
and gnaws
and the hours, days, weeks
years
seem wasted—
stretched there upon my bed
in the dark
looking upward at the ceiling
I get what many will consider an
obnoxious thought:
it's still nice to be
Bukowski.

the chemistry of things

I always thought Mary Lou was skinny and
not much to look at
while almost all the other guys
thought she was a
hot number.
maybe that's why she hung around me
in Jr. High.
my indifference must have attracted
her.

I was cool and mean in those days
and when the guys asked me,
"you banged Mary Lou yet?"
I answered them with the
truth: "she
bores me."

there was this guy
he taught chemistry.
Mr. Humm. Humm wore a little bow
tie and a black coat, a
cheap wrinkled job, he was
supposed to have
brains

and one day Mary Lou came to
me
and said Humm kept her
after class
and had taken her into the
closet and
kissed her and
fondled her

panties.
she was crying, "what will I
do?"

"forget it," I told her,
"those chemicals have scrambled
his brain. we have an English teacher
who hikes her skirt up around her
hips every day and wants to go to bed with
every guy in class. we enjoy her but
ignore her."

"why don't you beat Mr. Humm up?"
she asked me.

"I could but they'd transfer me to
Stuart Hall."

in Stuart Hall they beat the shit
out of you
and they ignored math, English,
music, they just stuck you into auto
shop
where you fixed up old cars
which they resold at big
profits.

"I thought you cared for me," said Mary
Lou, "don't you realize he
kissed me, stuck his tongue down my
throat and had his hand up my
behind?"

"well," I said, "we saw Mrs. Lattimore's
pussy the other day, in English."

Mary Lou walked off
crying . . .

well, she told her
mother and Humm got his, he
had to
resign, poor son of a
bitch.

after that the guys asked me,
"hey, what do you think of Humm
sticking his hand up your girl's
ass?"

"just another guy with no
taste," I answered.

I was cool and mean
in those days and I went on to
high school, the same one
Mary Lou attended
where she secretly got
married
during her senior year
to a guy
I knew, a guy I
outdrank and beat the shit out of
a couple of
times.

the guy thought he had
something.
he wanted me to be
best man.

I told him, no thanks and lots of
luck.

I never could see what
they saw in
Mary Lou.
and poor Humm: what a
lonely sick old
fart.

anyhow, then I went on to
city college
where the only molesting I
could see going on
was what they did to your
mind.

rift

"I can't live with you anymore,"
she said,
"*look* at you!"

"uuh?" I
asked.

"*look* at you!
sitting in that god
damned
chair!
your belly is sticking out
of your
underwear,
you've burnt cigarette
holes in all your
shirts!
all you *do* is suck
on that god damned
beer,
bottle after bottle,
what do you get out of
that?"

"the damage has been
done," I told
her.

"what're you talking
about?"

"nothing matters and
we know nothing matters

and *that*
matters . . ."

"you're drunk!"

"come on, baby, let's get
along, it's
easy . . ."

"not for *me*!" she screamed,
"not for
me!"

she ran into the bathroom to
put on her
makeup.
I got up for another
beer.
I sat back down
just had the new bottle
to my mouth
when she came out of the
bathroom.

"holy shit!" she screamed,
"you're
disgusting!"

I laughed right into the
bottle, gagged, spit a mouthful of
beer across my
undershirt.

"my god!" she
said.

she slammed the door and
was gone.

I looked at the closed door
and at the doorknob
and strangely
I didn't feel
alone.

my friend, the parking lot attendant

—he's a dandy
—small black mustache
—usually sucking on a cigar

he tends to lean into the cars as he
transacts business

first time I met him, he said,
"hey! ya gonna make a
killin'?"

"maybe," I answered.

next meeting it was:
"hey, Ramrod! what's
happening?"

"very little," I told
him.

next time I had my girlfriend with me
and he just
grinned.

next time I was
alone.

"hey," he asked, "where's the young
chick?"

"I left her at home . . ."

"*Bullshit*! I'll bet she dumped
you!"

and the next time
he really leaned into the car:

"what's a guy like *you* doing driving a
BMW? I'll bet you inherited your
money, you didn't get this car with your
brains!"

"how'd you guess?" I
answered.

that was some weeks ago.
I haven't seen him lately.
fellow like that, chances are he just moved on
to better
things.

miracle

I have just listened to this
symphony which Mozart dashed off
in one day
and it had enough wild and crazy
joy to last
forever,
whatever forever
is
Mozart came as close as
possible to
that.

a non-urgent poem

I had this fellow write me that
he felt there wasn't the
"urgency" in my poems
of the present
as compared to my poems
of the past.

now, if this *is* true
why did he write me
about it?
have I made his days
more
incomplete?
it's
possible.

well, I too have felt
let down
by writers
I once thought were
powerful
or
at least
very damned
good
but
I never considered
writing them to
inform them that I
sensed their
demise.
I found the best thing
I could do

was just to type away
at my own work
and let the dying
die
as they always
have.

my first affair with that older woman

when I look back now
at the abuse I took from
her
I feel shame that I was so
innocent,
but I must say
she did match me drink for
drink,
and I realized that her life
her feelings for things
had been ruined
along the way
and that I was no more than a
temporary
companion;
she was ten years older
and mortally hurt by the past
and the present;
she treated me badly:
desertion, other
men;
she brought me immense
pain,
continually;
she lied, stole;
there was desertion,
other men,
yet we had our moments; and
our little soap opera ended
with her in a coma
in the hospital,
and I sat at her bed
for hours

talking to her,
and then she opened her eyes
and saw me:
"I knew it would be you,"
she said.
then she closed her
eyes.

the next day she was
dead.

I drank alone
for two years
after that.

the freeway life

some fool kept blocking me and I finally got around him, and
    in the
elation of freedom I ran it up to 85 (naturally, first checking
    the rear
view for our blue suited protectors); then I felt and heard the
    SMASH of a hard
object upon the bottom of my car, but wanting to make the
    track I willed
myself to ignore it (as if that would make it vanish) even
    though I began
to smell gasoline.
I checked the gas gauge and it *seemed* to be holding . . .

it had been a terrible week already
but, you know, defeat can strengthen just as victory can
    weaken, and if
you have the proper luck and the holy endurance the gods just
    might deliver
the proper admixture . . .
then
traffic backed up and stopped, and then I really smelled gas and
    I saw my
gas gauge dipping rapidly, then my radio told me that a man
3 miles up
on the Vernon overpass had one leg over the side and was
    threatening
suicide,
and there I was threatened with being blown to hell
as people yelled at me that my tank was broken and pouring
    gasoline;
yes, I nodded back, I know, I know . . .
meanwhile, waving cars off and working my way over to the
    outer lane

thinking, they are more terrorized than I am:
if I go, those nearby might go also.

there was no motion in the traffic—the suicide was still trying
    to make
up his mind and my gas gauge dipped into the red
and then the necessity of being a proper citizen and waiting for
    opportunity
vanished and I made my move
up and over a cement abutment
bending my right front wheel
I made it to the freeway exit which was totally
clear
then worked on down to a gas station on Imperial Highway
parked it
still dripping gas, got out, made it to the phone, got in a call
for the tow truck, not a long wait at all, nice drive back in
    with a black
fellow who told me strange stories about stranded
    motorists . . .
(like one woman, her hands were frozen to the wheel, took 15
    minutes of
talking and prying to make her let go.)

had the car back in a couple of days, was driving back from the
    track,
hit the brake and it wouldn't go down, luckily I wasn't on the
    freeway
yet, cut the ignition, glided to the curb, noted that the steering
column cover had ripped loose and blocked the brake, ripped
    that away, then
ripped some more to make sure, then a whole mass of wires
    spilled out,
s h i t . . .
I turned the key, hit the gas but the car STARTED
and I drove off with the dangling wires against my leg

thinking
do these things happen to other
people or am
I just the chosen one?
I decided it was the latter and got onto the freeway where
some guy in a volks swung over and blocked my
lane
whereupon I swung around the son-of-a-bitch and hit
75, 80, 85 . . .
thinking, the courage it took to get out of bed each
morning
to face the same things
over and over
was
enormous.

the player

I had 40 win on the 6 horse
he had 2 lengths in the stretch
was running along the rail
when the jock whipped him
right-handed
and the horse hit the wood
spilled
threw the jock
and there went the race
for me.

that was the 7th race
and I considered that the horse
might have lost
anyhow
and then I considered leaving
but I decided to play the
8th,
hit 20 win on a 5 to one
shot.

in the 9th I went 40 win
on the second favorite
and when the bell rang to start them
the horse reared and
left my jock
in the stall.

I took the escalator down
and walked out the
gate
where a young man asked me
for a dollar so he could

take the bus
home.

I gave him the buck and
told him,
"you ought to stay away from this
place."

"yeah," he said, "I
know."

then I walked toward parking
searching my coat for
cigarettes.

nothing.

p.o. box 11946, Fresno, Calif. 93776

drove in from the track after losing $50.
a hot day out there
they pack them in on a Saturday;
my feet hurt and I had pains in the neck
and about the shoulders —
nerves: large crowds of people more than
unsettle me.
pulled into the driveway and got the
mail
moved up and parked it
went in and opened the IRS letter
form 525 (SC) (Rev. 9-83)
read it
and was informed that I owed
TWELVE THOUSAND SIXHUNDREDFOUR DOLLARS
        AND
SEVENTY EIGHT CENTS
on my 1981 income tax plus
TWO THOUAND EIGHTHUNDREDEIGHTYTHREE
        DOLLARS
AND TWELVE CENTS interest
and that further interest was being
compounded
DAILY.
I went into the kitchen and poured a
drink.
life in America was a curious
thing.
well, I *could* let the interest
build
that's what the government
did
but after a while they would

come for me
or whatever I had
left.
at least that $50 loss at the
track didn't look so
bad anymore.
I'd have to go tomorrow and
win $15,487.90 plus
daily compounded
interest.
I drank to that,
wishing I had purchased a
Racing Form
on the way
out.

poor Al

I don't know how he does it
but every woman he meets is
crazy.
he will get rid of one
crazy woman
but he never gets any
relief—
another crazy moves right in
with him.

it's only after they move in
and begin acting
more than strange
that they admit to him
that they've done madhouse
time
or that their families have
a long history of mental
illness.

his last one
he sent to a shrink
once a week:
$75 for 45 minutes.
after 7 months
she walked out on the
shrink
and said to Al,
"that god damned fag doesn't know
anything."

I don't know how they all find
Al.

he says you can't tell at the first
meeting
they have their guard up
but after 2 or 3 months the
guard comes down
and there's Al with
another one.

It got so bad that Al thought
maybe it was
him
so he went to a shrink
and asked
and the shrink said,
"you're one of the sanest men
I've ever met."

poor Al.

that made him feel
worse
than ever.

for my ivy league friends:

many of those I met on the reading circuit or heard about on
    the reading
circuit in the old days are now either teaching or poets-in-
    residence
and have garnered Guggenheims and N.E.A.'s and sundry other
    grants.
well, I tried for a Gugg once myself, even got an N.E.A. so I
    can't
knock the act
but
you should have seen them back then: raggedy-ass, wild-eyed,
    raving
against the order
now
they have been ingested, digested, rested
they write reviews for the journals
they write well-worked, quiet, inoffensive poesy
they edit so many of the magazines that I have no idea where I
    should send this
poem
since they attack my work with alarming regularity
and
I can't read theirs
yet their attacks upon me have been effective in this country
and
if it weren't for Europe I'd probably still be a starving writer
or down at the row
or diggin weeds out of your garden
or . . . ?

well
you know the old saying: it's all a matter of
taste

and
either they're right and I'm wrong or I'm right and they're all
wrong
or
maybe it's some place in between.
most of the people in the world could care less
and
I often feel the same
way.

helping the old

I was standing in line at the bank today
when the old fellow in front of me
dropped his glasses (luckily, within the
case)
and as he bent over
I saw how difficult it was for
him
and I said, "wait, let me get
them . . ."
but as I picked them up
he dropped his cane
a beautiful, black polished
cane
and I got the glasses back to him
then went for the cane
steadying the old boy
as I handed him his cane.
he didn't speak,
he just smiled at me.
then he turned
forward.

I stood behind him waiting
my turn.

bad times at the 3rd and Vermont hotel

Alabam was a sneak and a thief and he came to my
room when I was drunk and
each time I got up he shoved me back
down.

you prick, I told him, you know I can
take you!

he just shoved me down
again.

when I sober up, I said, I'm going to kick you
all the way to hell!

he just kept pushing me
around.

I finally caught him a good one, right over the
temple
and he backed off and
left.

it was a couple of days later
I got even: I fucked his
girl.

then I went down and knocked on his
door.

well, Alabam, I fucked your woman and now I'm going to
kick you all the way to
hell!

the poor guy started crying, he put his hands over his
face and just cried

I stood there and watched
him.

I said, I'm sorry,
Alabam.

then I left him there, I went back to
my room.

we were all alkies and none of us had jobs, all we had
was each other.

even then, my so-called woman was in some bar or
somewhere, I hadn't seen her in a couple of
days.

I had a bottle of port
left.

I uncorked it and took it down to Alabam's
room.

said, how about a drink,
Rebel?

he looked up, stood up, went for two
glasses.

the Master Plan

starving in a Philadelphia winter
trying to be a writer
I wrote and wrote and drank and drank and
drank
and then stopped writing and concentrated on
the drinking.

it was another
art-form.

if you can't have any luck with one thing you
try another.

of course, I had been practicing on the
drinking-form
since the age of
15.

and there was much competition
in that field
also.

it was a world full of drunks and writers and
drunk writers.

and so
I became a starving drunk instead of a starving
writer.

the best thing was the instant
result.
and I soon became the biggest and
best drunk in the neighborhood and

maybe the whole
city.

it sure as hell beat sitting around waiting for
those rejection slips from *The New Yorker* and *The
Atlantic Monthly.*

of course, I never really considered quitting the
writing game, I just wanted to give it a
ten year rest
figuring if I got famous too early
I wouldn't have anything left for the stretch run
like I have now, thank
you,

with the drinking still thrown
in.

garbage

I had taken a tremendous beating,
I had chosen a real bull, and because of
the girls and for himself and just because of his
brutal escaping energy
he had almost murdered me:
I learned later
that even after I was out
he had kicked my head again and
again
and then had emptied several garbage cans
over me
and then they had left me there
in that alley.
I was the guy from out of town.

it was around 6 a.m. on a Sunday
morning when I came
around.
my face was a mass of
bruises, scabs, clots, bumps, lumps, my lips
thick and numb, my eyes almost swollen
shut
but I got to my feet and began
walking;
I could see traces of the sun, houses, the shaking
sidewalk as I
moved toward my room
then I heard shuffling sounds from the
center of the street
and I forced my eyes to
focus and saw this
man staggering
his clothing ripped and bloody

he smelled of death and darkness
but he kept moving forward
down the middle of the street
as if he had been walking for
miles
from some event so ugly that
the mind itself might refuse to accept it
as part of life.
my impulse was to help him
and I stepped off the
curbing
and moved toward him.
he couldn't see me, he moved forward
looking for somewhere to go,
anywhere, and
I saw one of his eyes hanging
out of the socket,
dangling.
I backed away.
he was like a creature not of the
earth.
I let him go
by.
I heard him moving away
behind me
those blind steps
lurching, in
agony,
senselessly
alone.

I got back on the
sidewalk.
I got back to my
room.
I got myself to the

bed.
fell face up
the ceiling up there above me,
I waited.

my vanishing act

when I got sick of the bar
and I sometimes did
I had a place to go:
it was a tall field of grass
an abandoned
graveyard.
I didn't consider this to be a
morbid pastime.
it just seemed to be the best
place to be.
it offered a generous cure to
the vicious hangover.
through the grass I could see
the stones,
many were tilted
at strange angles
against gravity
as though they must
fall
but I never saw one
fall
although there were many of those
in the yard.
it was cool and dark
with a breeze
and I often slept
there.
I was never
bothered.

each time I returned to the bar
after an absence
it was always the same with

them:
"where the hell you
been? we thought you
died!"

I was their bar freak, they needed me
to make themselves feel
better.
just like, at times, I needed that
graveyard.

let's make a deal

in conjunction with
these rivers of shit
that keep rolling through my brain, Captain
Walrus, I can only say that I hardly understand
it and would say
any number of HAIL MARYS
to put a stop to it—
I'd even go back to living with that whore with the
heart of brass just
to keep these rivers of shit from rolling through my
brain, Captain Walrus, but
of course
I would never stop playing the horses or
drinking
but
Captain
to keep these rivers from flowing
I'd promise to never
eat eggs again and
I'd shave my head and my balls, I'd live in
the state of Delaware and I'd even
force myself to sit through any movie acted in by
any member of the Fonda
family.

think about it, Captain Walrus, the
plum is in the pudding and the parasol bends to
the West wind
I've got to do something about all
this . . .
it seems like it never
stops.

each man's hell is in a different
place: mine is just up and
behind
my ruined
face.

16-bit Intel 8088 chip

with an Apple Macintosh
you can't run Radio Shack programs
in its disc drive.
nor can a Commodore 64
drive read a file
you have created on an
IBM Personal Computer.
both Kaypro and Osborne computers use
the CP/M operating system
but can't read each other's
handwriting
for they format (write
on) discs in different
ways.
the Tandy 2000 runs MS-DOS but
can't use most programs produced for
the IBM Personal Computer
unless certain
bits and bytes are
altered
but the wind still blows over
Savannah
and in the Spring
the turkey buzzard struts and
flounces before his
hens.

zero

sitting here watching the second hand on the TIMEX go
    around and
around . . .
this will hardly be a night to remember
sitting here searching for blackheads on the back of my neck
as other men enter the sheets with dolls of flame
I look into myself and find perfect emptiness.
I am out of cigarettes and don't even have a gun to point.
this writer's block is my only possession.
the second hand on the TIMEX still goes around and
around . . .
I always wanted to be a writer
now I'm one who can't.

might as well go downstairs and watch late night tv with the
    wife
she'll ask me how it went
I'll wave a hand nonchalantly
settle down next to her
and watch the glass people fail
as I have failed.

I'm going to walk down the stairway now

what a sight:

an empty man being careful not to trip and bang his empty
head.

putrefaction

of late
I've had this thought
that this country
has gone backwards
4 or 5 decades
and that all the
social advancement
the good feeling of
person toward
person
has been washed
away
and replaced by the same
old
bigotries.

we have
more than ever
the selfish wants of power
the disregard for the
weak
the old
the impoverished
the
helpless.

we are replacing want with
war
salvation with
slavery.

we have wasted the
gains

we have become
rapidly
less.

we have our Bomb
it is our fear
our damnation
and our
shame.

now
something so sad
has hold of us
that
the breath
leaves
and we can't even
cry.

I'll take it . . .

maybe I'm going crazy, that's all right
but these poems keep rising to the top of my
head with more and more
force. now
after the oceans of booze that I have
consumed
it would only seem that attrition would
be my rightful reward as I continue to
consume—while
the madhouses, skidrows and graveyards are
filled with the likes of
me—
yet each night as I sit down to this machine
with my bottle
the poems flare and jump out, on and
on—roaring in the glee of
easy power: 65 years
dancing—my mouth curling into a
tiny grin
as these keys keep meting out a
substantial energy of cock-
eyed miracle.

the gods have been kind to me through this
life-style that would have killed
an ox of a man
and I'm no ox of a
man.

I sensed from the beginning, of
course, that there was a strange gnawing
inside of me

but I never dreamed this
luck
this absolute shot of
grace

my death will at most seem
an
afterthought.

supposedly famous

not much to hang onto in this early morning growling,
my wife, poor dear, downstairs,
I am at the racetrack all day and
up here all night with the bottle and
this machine.
my wife, poor dear, may she find her place
in heaven.

then too
the few people that I have
known, the people I thought had that
little extra flare
that inventive humanity, well, they
dissolved
but
being a natural loner
I am not over-
distraught —
there are still my 5
cats: Ting, Ding, Beeker, Bleeker and
Blob.
not much to hang on to in this early morning growling.
I am now a
supposedly famous
writer
influencing hordes of
typists.
would
that I could
laugh
at all
this.

Fame is the last whore, all the others are
gone.

well, the competition ain't been
much
but that's no hair off my
wrists: I realized all that
long ago while
starving and
pissing out the
window
while smashing waterglasses of
booze against the behind-in-the-
rent
walls.

Ting, Ding, Beeker, Bleeker and
Blob.

now Death is a plant growing in my
mind

not much to hang on to in this early morning growling.

I am sad for the dead and I am sad for the living
but not for my 5 cats or
for my wife, my wife who will
find her place in
heaven.

and as for the people
dissolved
I didn't dissolve them, they dissolved
themselves.

and that the sidewalks are empty while
full of feet
passing—
this is the working of the
way.
not much to hang on to
as
a man plays a piano
through my radio and
the walls
stand up and
down

as the courage of everything
even the fleas
the lice
the tarantula
astounds me
in this early morning
growling.

the last shot

here we are, once again, the last drink, the last
poem—decades of this splendid luck—another drunken
a.m., and not on the drunktank floor tonight waiting for
the black pimp to get off the phone so I can put through my
    one
allowed call (so many of those a.m.s too) it took
me a long time to find the most interesting person to
drink with: myself, like this, now reaching to my left
for the last glass of the Blood of the
Lamb.

whorehouse

my first experience in a whorehouse
was in Tijuana.
it was a large place on the edge of
the city.
I was 17, with two friends.
we got drunk to get our guts
up
then went on
in.
the place was packed with
servicemen
mostly
sailors.
the sailors stood in long
lines
hollering, and beating on
the doors.

Lance got in a short
line (the lines indicated the
age of the whore: the shorter the
line the older the
whore)
and got it over
with, came out bold and
grinning: "well, what you guys
waiting for?"

the other guy, Jack, he passed me
the tequila bottle and I took a
hit and passed it back and he
took a hit.

Lance looked at us: "I'll be
in the car, sleeping it
off."

Jack and I waited until he was
gone
then started walking toward the
exit.
Jack was wearing this big
sombrero
and right at the exit was an
old whore sitting in a
chair.
she stuck out her leg
barring our
way: "come on, boys, I'll make
it *good* for you and
cheap!"

somehow that scared the
shit out of Jack and he
said, "my god, I'm going to
PUKE!"

"NOT ON THE FLOOR!" screamed
the whore
and with that
Jack ripped off his
sombrero
and holding it
before him
he must have puked a
gallon.

then he just stood there
staring down

at it
and the whore
said, "get out of
here!"

Jack ran out the door with
his sombrero
and then the whore
got a very kind look upon her
face and said to me:
"*cheap!*" and I walked
into a room with her
and there was a big fat man
sitting in a chair and
I asked her, "who's
that?"
and she said, "he's here to
see that I don't get
hurt."

and I walked over to the
man and said, "hey, how ya
doin'?"

and he said, "fine,
señor . . ."

and I said,
"you live around
here?"

and he said, "give
her the
money."

"how much?"

"two dollars."

I gave the lady the two
dollars
then walked back to the
man.

"I might come and live
in Mexico some day," I
told him.

"get the hell out of
here," he said,
"NOW!"

as I walked through the
exit
Jack was waiting out there
without his
sombrero
but he was still
wavering
drunk.

"Christ," I said, "she was
great, she actually got my
balls into her
mouth!"

we walked back to the car.
Lance was passed out, we
awakened him and he drove us
out of
there

somehow
we got through the border
crossing

and all the way
driving back to
L.A.

we rode Jack for being a
chickenshit
virgin.
Lance did it in a gentle
manner
but I was loud
demeaning Jack for his lack of
guts
and I kept at it
until Jack passed out
near
San Clemente.

I sat up there next to
Lance as we passed the last
tequila bottle back and
forth.

as Los Angeles rushed toward
us
Jack asked, "how was
it?"
and I answered
in a worldly
tone: "I've had
better."

starting fast

we each
at times
should
remember
the most
elevated
and
lucky
moment
of
our
lives.

for me
it
was
being
a
very young
man
and
sleeping
penniless
and
friendless
upon a
park
bench
in a
strange
city

which
doesn't say
much
for all
those
many
decades
which
followed.

the crazy truth

the nut in the red outfit
came walking down the street
talking to himself
when a hotshot in a sports car
cut into an alley
in front of the nut
who hollered, "HEY, DOG DRIP!
SWINE SHIT! YOU GOT PEANUTS FOR
BRAINS?"

the hotshot braked his sports
car, backed toward the nut,
stopped,
said: "WHAT'S THAT YOU SAID,
BUDDY?"

"I said, YOU BETTER
DRIVE OFF WHILE YOU CAN,
ASSHOLE!"

the hotshot had his girl in the
car with him and started to
open the door.

"YOU BETTER NOT GET OUT OF THAT
CAR, PEANUT BRAIN!"

the door closed and the sports car
roared
off.

the nut in the red outfit then
continued to walk down the
street.

"THERE AIN'T NOTHIN' NOWHERE,"
he said, "AND IT'S GETTING TO BE
LESS THAN NOTHING ALL THE
TIME!"

it was a great day
there on 7th Street just off
Weymouth
Drive.

drive through hell

the people are weary, unhappy and frustrated, the people are
bitter and vengeful, the people are deluded and fearful, the
people are angry and uninventive
and I drive among them on the freeway and they project
what is left of themselves in their manner of driving—
some more hateful, more thwarted than others—
some don't like to be passed, some attempt to keep others
from passing
—some attempt to block lane changes
—some hate cars of a newer, more expensive model
—others in these cars hate the older cars.

the freeway is a circus of cheap and petty emotions, it's
humanity on the move, most of them coming from some place
        they
hated and going to another they hate just as much or
more.
the freeways are a lesson in what we have become and
most of the crashes and deaths are the collision
of incomplete beings, of pitiful and demented
lives.

when I drive the freeways I see the soul of humanity of
my city and it's ugly, ugly, ugly: the living have choked the
heart
away.

for the concerned:

if you get married they think you're
finished
and if you are without a woman they think you're
incomplete.

a large portion of my readers want me to
keep writing about bedding down with madwomen and
streetwalkers—
also, about being in jails and hospitals, or
starving or
puking my guts
out.

I agree that complacency hardly engenders an
immortal literature
but neither does
repetition.

for those readers now
sick at heart
believing that I'm a contented
man—
please have some
cheer: agony sometimes changes
form
but
it never ceases for
anybody.

a funny guy

Schopenhauer couldn't abide the masses,
they drove him mad
but he was able to say,
"at least, I am not them."
and this consoled him to some
extent
and I think one of his most humorous writings
was when he expostulated against some man who
uselessly cracked his whip
over his horse
completely destroying a thought process
Arthur was involved
in.

but the man with the whip was a part of the
whole
no matter how seemingly useless and
stupid
and once great thoughts
often with time
become useless and
stupid.

but Schopenhauer's rage was so
beautiful
so well placed that I laughed
out loud
then
put him down
next to Nietzsche
who was also
all too
human.

shoes

when you're young
a pair of
female
high-heeled shoes
just sitting
alone
in the closet
can fire your
bones;
when you're old
it's just
a pair of shoes
without
anybody
in them
and
just as
well.

coffee

I was having a coffee at the
counter
when a man
3 or 4 stools down
asked me,
"listen, weren't you the
guy who was
hanging from his
heels
from that 4th floor
hotel room
the other
night?"

"yes," I answered, "that
was me."

"what made you do
that?" he asked.

"well, it's pretty
involved."

he looked away
then.

the waitress
who had been
standing there
asked me,
"he was joking,
wasn't
he?"

"no," I
said.

I paid, got up, walked
to the door, opened
it.

I heard the man
say, "that guy's
nuts."

out on the street I
walked north
feeling
curiously
honored.

together

HEY, I hollered across the
room to her,
DRINK SOME WINE OUT OF
YOUR SHOE!

WHY? she
screamed.

BECAUSE THIS USELESSNESS
NEEDS SOME
GAMBLE!
I yelled
back.

HEY, the guy in the next
apartment beat on the
wall, I'VE GOT TO GET UP
IN THE MORNING AND GO
TO WORK SO FOR CHRIST'S
SAKE, SHUT
UP!

he damn near broke the wall
down and had a most
powerful
voice.

I walked over to
her, said, listen, let's
be quiet, he's got some
rights.

FUCK YOU, YOU ASSHOLE!
she screamed
at me.

the guy began pounding
on the wall
again.

she was right and he was
right.

I walked the bottle over
to the window and
looked out into the
night.

then I had a good roaring
drink
and I thought, we are all
doomed
together, that's all there is
to
it. (that's all there was
to that particular drink, just
like all the
others.)

then I walked
back to her and
she was asleep in
her
chair.

I carried her to
the bed
turned out the

lights
then sat in the
chair by the
window
sucking at the
bottle, thinking,
well, I've gotten
this far
and that's
plenty.

and now
she's sleeping
and
maybe
he can
too.

the finest of the breed

there's nothing to
discuss
there's nothing to
remember
there's nothing to
forget

it's sad
and
it's not
sad

seems the
most sensible
thing
a person can
do
is
sit
with drink in
hand
as the walls
wave
their goodbye
smiles

one comes through
it
all
with a certain
amount of
efficiency and

bravery
then
leaves

some accept
the possibility of
God
to help them
get
through

others
take it
straight on

and to these

I drink
tonight.

close to greatness

at one stage in my life
I met a man who claimed to have
visited Pound at St. Elizabeths.

then I met a woman who not only
claimed to have visited
E.P.
but also to have made love
to him — she even showed
me
certain sections in the
Cantos
where Ezra was supposed to have
mentioned
her.

so there was this man and
this woman
and the woman told me
that Pound had never
mentioned a visit from this
man
and the man claimed that the
lady had had nothing to do
with the
master
that she was a
charlatan.

and since I wasn't a
Poundian scholar
I didn't know who to
believe

but
one thing I do
know: when a man is
living
many claim relationships
that are hardly
so
and after he dies, well,
then it's everybody's
party.

my guess is that Pound
knew neither the lady or the
gentleman

or if he knew
one
or if he knew
both

it was a shameful waste of
madhouse
time.

the stride

Norman and I, both 19, striding the streets of
night . . . feeling big, young young, big and
young

Norman said, "Jesus Christ, I bet nobody
walks with giant strides like we do!"

1939
after having listened to
Stravinsky

not long
after,
the war got
Norman.

I sit here now
46 years later
on the second floor of a hot
one a.m. morning

drunk

still big
not
so young.

Norman, you would
never guess
what
has happened to

me
what
has happened to
all of
us.
I remember your
saying: "make it or
break it."

neither happened and
it
won't.

final story

god, there he is drunk again
telling the same old stories
over and over again
as they push him for
more—some with nothing
else to do, others
secretly snickering
at this
great writer
babbling
drooling
in his little white
rat
whiskers
talking about
war
talking about the
wars
talking about the brave
fish
the bullfights
even about his wives.

the people
come into the
bar
night after night
for the same old
show
which he will one day
end
alone

blowing his brains to
the walls.

the price of creation
is never
too high.

the price of living
with other people
always
is.

friends within the darkness

I can remember starving in a
small room in a strange city
shades pulled down, listening to
classical music
I was young I was so young it hurt like a knife
inside
because there was no alternative except to hide as long
as possible—
not in self-pity but with dismay at my limited chance:
trying to connect.

the old composers—Mozart, Bach, Beethoven,
Brahms were the only ones who spoke to me and
they were dead.

finally, starved and beaten, I had to go into
the streets to be interviewed for low-paying and
monotonous
jobs
by strange men behind desks
men without eyes men without faces
who would take my hours
break them
piss on them.

now I work for the editors the readers the
critics

but still hang around and drink with
Mozart, Bach, Brahms and the
Bee
some buddies
some men

sometimes all we need to be able to continue alone
are the dead
rattling the walls
that close us in.

death sat on my knee and cracked with laughter

I was writing three short stories a week
and sending them to the *Atlantic Monthly*
they would all come back.
my money went for stamps and envelopes
and paper and wine
and I got so thin I used to
suck my cheeks
together
and they'd meet over the top of my
tongue (that's when I thought about
Hamsun's *Hunger* — where he ate his own
flesh; I once took a bite of my wrist
but it was very salty).

anyhow, one night in Miami Beach (I
have no idea what I was doing in that
city) I had not eaten in 60 hours
and I took the last of my starving
pennies
went down to the corner grocery and
bought a loaf of bread.
I planned to chew each slice slowly —
as if each were a slice of turkey
or a luscious
steak
and I got back to my room and
opened the wrapper and the
slices of bread were green
and mouldy.

my party was not to be.

I just dumped the bread upon the
floor
and I sat on that bed wondering about
the green mould, the
decay.

my rent money was used up and
I listened to all the sounds
of all the people in that
roominghouse

and down on the floor were
the dozens of stories with the
dozens of *Atlantic Monthly*
rejection slips.

it was early evening and I
turned out the light and
went to bed and
it wasn't long before I
heard the mice coming out,
I heard them creeping over my
immortal stories and
eating the
green mouldy bread.

and in the morning
when I awakened
I saw that
all that was left of the
bread
was the green
mould.
they had eaten right to the
edge of the mould
leaving chunks of

it
among the stories and
rejection slips
as I heard the sound of
my landlady's vacuum
cleaner
bumping down the
hall
slowly approaching my
door.

oh yes

I've been so
down in the mouth
lately
that sometimes when I
bend over to
lace my shoes
there are
three
tongues.

O tempora! O mores!

I get these girly magazines in the mail because
I'm writing short stories for them again
and here in these pages are these ladies
exposing their jewel boxes—
it looks more like a gynecologist's
journal—
everything boldly and clinically
exposed
beneath bland and bored physiognomies.
it's a turn-off of gigantic
proportions:
the secret is in the
imagination—
take that away and you have dead
meat.

a century back
a man could be driven mad
by a well-turned
ankle, and
why not?
one could imagine
that the rest
would be
magical
indeed!

now they shove it at us like a
McDonald's hamburger
on a platter.

there is hardly anything as beautiful as
a woman in a long dress

not even the sunrise
not even the geese flying south
in the long V formation
in the bright freshness
of early morning.

the passing of a great one

he was the only living writer I ever met who I truly
admired and he was dying when I met
him.
(we in this game are shy on praise even toward
those who do it very well, but I never had this
problem with J.F.)
I visited him several times at the
hospital (there was never anybody else
about) and upon entering his room
I was never sure if he was asleep
or?

"John?"

he was stretched there on that bed, blind
and amputated:
advanced
diabetes.

"John it's
Hank . . ."

he would answer and then we would talk for
a short bit (mostly he would talk and I would
listen; after all, he was our mentor, our
god):

Ask the Dust
Wait Until Spring, Bandini
Dago Red

all the others.

to end up in Hollywood writing
movie scripts
that's what killed
him.

"the worst thing," he told me,
"is bitterness, people end up so
bitter."

he wasn't bitter, although he had
every right to
be . . .

at the funeral I
met several of his script-writing
buddies.

"let's write something about
John," one of them
suggested.

"I don't think I can," I
told them.

and, of course, they never
did.

the wine of forever

re-reading some of Fante's
The Wine of Youth
in bed
this mid-afternoon
my big cat
BEAKER
asleep beside
me.

the writing of some
men
is like a vast bridge
that carries you
over
the many things
that claw and tear.

Fante's pure and magic
emotions
hang on the simple
clean
line.

that this man died
one of the slowest and
most horrible deaths
that I ever witnessed or
heard
about . . .

the gods play no
favorites.

I put the book down
beside me.

book on one side,
cat on the
other . . .

John, meeting you,
even the way it
was was the event of my
life. I can't say
I would have died for
you, I couldn't have handled
it that well.

but it was good to see you
again
this
afternoon.

true

one of Lorca's best lines
is,
"agony, always
agony . . ."

think of this when you
kill a
cockroach or
pick up a razor to
shave

or awaken in the morning
to
face the
sun.

Glenn Miller

long ago
across from the campus
in the malt shop
the juke box going
the young girls perfectly in tune
dancing with the football players
and the college bright boys

Glenn Miller was the big thing then
and everybody stepped
almost everybody
I sat with a couple of disciples
we were supposed to be outlaws
the explorers of Truth
but I liked the music
and the laziness of waiting
as the world rushed toward war
as Hitler speechified
the girls whirled
graceful
showing leg
that last bright sunshine
we warmed ourselves in it
shutting away everything else
while the universe opened its mouth
in an attempt to
swallow us all.

Emily Bukowski

my grandmother always attended the sunrise
Easter service
and the Rose Bowl
parade.

she also liked to go to the
beach, sit on those benches
facing the sea.

she thought movies were
sinful.

she ate enormous platefuls of
food.

she prayed for me
constantly.

"poor boy: the devil is inside
of you."

she said the devil was
inside her husband
too.

though not divorced
they lived
separately
and had not seen each
other
for 15 years.

she said that hospitals were
nonsense

she never used them
or
the doctors.

at 87
she died one evening
while feeding her
canary.

she liked to
drop the seed
into the cage
while making these
little
bird sounds.

she wasn't very
interesting
but few people
are.

some suggestions

in addition to the envy and the rancor of some of
my peers
there is the other thing, it comes by telephone and
letter: "you are the world's greatest living
writer."

this doesn't please me either because somehow
I believe that to be the world's greatest living
writer
there must be something
terribly wrong with you.

I don't even want to be the world's greatest
dead writer.

just being dead would be fair
enough.

also, the word "writer" is a very tiresome
word.

just think how much more pleasing it would be
to hear:
you are the world's greatest pool
player
or
you are the world's greatest
fucker
or
you are the world's greatest
horseplayer.

now
that
would really make
a man feel
good.

invasion

I didn't know that
there was anything
in the closet
although some nights
my sleep would be
interrupted by strange
rumblings
but
I always thought
these to be
minor
quakes.

the closet was
the one
down the hall
and
was seldom
used.

the curious thing
for me
was that
the cats
(I had 4 of
them)
appeared to be
leaving
large
droppings
about
(and

they were
house-broken).

then
the cats
vanished
one by
one
but the fresh
droppings
kept
appearing.

it was one night
while I was
reading the
stock market
quotations
that I
looked up

and
there stood
the
lion
in the bedroom
doorway.

I was
in bed
propped up
with a
couple of
pillows
and drinking a

hot
chocolate.

now
nobody
can believe
a lion
in a
bedroom —
at least
not
in a city
of any
size.

so
I just kept
looking at the
lion
and not
quite
believing.

then
it turned and
walked down the
stairway.

I
followed it —
a good
18 feet
behind —
clutching my
baseball bat

in one
hand
and my
4-inch knife
in the
other.

I watched the
lion
go down the
stairway
then walk
across the front
room

it paused
before the large
plate glass
sliding
doors
which faced the
yard and the
street.

they were
closed.

the lion
emitted an
impatient
growl

and
leaped through the
glass

crashing through
into the
night.

I sat
on the couch
in the
dark
still unable
to believe
what
I had
seen.

then
I heard
a scream
of such utter
agony and
terror
that
for a
moment
I could
neither
see
breathe nor
comprehend.

I rose,
turned to
barricade myself
in the
bedroom

only to see
3 small
lion cubs
trundling
down
the stairway —
cute
devilish
felines

as the
mother
returned
through the
night and the
shattered glass
door

half dragging
half carrying
a bloodied
man
across the
rug
leaving a
red
trail

the cubs
rushed
forward
and the
moon
came through
to light

the
whirling
feast.

hard times

as I got out of my car down at the docks
two men started walking toward
me.
one looked old and mean and the other was
big and smiling.
they were both wearing
caps.
they kept walking toward me.
I got ready.

"something bothering you guys?"

"no," said the old
guy.
they both stopped.
"don't you remember us?"

"I'm not sure . . ."

"we painted your house."

"oh, yeah . . . come on, I'll buy you a
beer . . ."

we walked toward a cafe.

"you were one of the nicest guys we ever
worked for . . ."

"yeah?"

"yeah, you kept bringing us beer . . ."

we sat at one of those rough tables
overlooking the harbor. we
sucked at our
beers.

"you still live with that young
woman?" asked the old
guy.

"yeah. how you guys doing?"

"there's no work now . . ."

I took out a ten and handed it to the old
one.

"listen, I forgot to tip you guys . . ."

"thanks."

we sat with our beer.
the canneries had shut down.
Todd Shipyard had failed
and was
phasing them
out.
San Pedro was back in the
30's.

I finished my beer.

"well, you guys, I gotta go."

"where ya gonna go?"

"gonna buy some fish . . ."

I walked off toward the fish market,
turned halfway there
gave them
thumb-up
right hand.

they both took their caps off and
waved them.
I laughed, turned, walked
off.

sometimes it's hard to know
what to
do.

longshot

of course, I had lost much blood
maybe it was a different kind of
dying
but I still had enough left to wonder
about
the absence of fear.

it was going to be easy: they had
put me in a special ward they had
in that place
for the poor who were
dying.
—the doors were a little thicker
—the windows a little smaller
and there was much
wheeling in and out of
bodies
plus
the presence of the priest
giving last
rites.

you saw the priest all the time
but you seldom saw a
doctor.

it was always nice to see a
nurse—
they rather took the place of
angels
for those who
believed in that sort of
thing.

the priest kept bugging me.

"no offense, Father, but I'd
rather die without
it," I whispered.

"but on your entrance application you
stated 'Catholic.' "

"that was just to be
social . . ."

"my son, once a Catholic, always a
Catholic!"

"Father," I whispered, "that's not
true . . ."

the nicest thing about the place were
the Mexican girls who came in to
change the sheets, they giggled, they
joked with the dying and
they were
beautiful.

and the worst thing was
the Salvation Army Band who
came around at
5:30 a.m.
Easter Morning
and gave us the old
religious feeling—horns and drums
and all, much
brass and
pounding, tremendous volume

there were 40 or so
in that room
and that band
stiffened a good
10 or 15 of us by
6 a.m.

and they rolled them right out
to the morgue elevator
over to the west, a very
busy elevator.

I stayed in Death's waiting room for
3 days.
I watched them roll out close to
fifty.

they finally got tired of waiting
for me
and rolled me
out of there.

a nice black homosexual fellow
pushed me
along.

"you want to know the odds of
coming out of that ward?"
he asked.

"yeah."

"50 to one."

"hell,
got any
smokes?"

"no, but I can get you
some."

we rolled along
as the sun managed to come through the
wire-webbed windows
and I began to think of
that first drink when
I got
out.

concrete

he had set up the
reading

he was one of the foremost practitioners
of concrete poetry
and after I read I went
up there to where he
lived

his place was high in the
mountains and
we drank and looked out the large
window at very large
birds
flying about

gliding mostly

he said they were eagles
(he might have been putting me
on)

and his wife played the
piano

a bit of
Brahms

he didn't talk
much

he was a concrete
man

his wife was very
beautiful

and the way the eagles
glided

that was very beautiful
also

then it was twilight

then it was night

and you couldn't see the eagles
anymore

it had been an afternoon
reading

we drank until one
a.m.

then I got into my car
and drove the winding
narrow road

d
  o
    w
      n

I was too drunk to fear the
danger

when I got to my place I
drank two bottles of

beer and went to
bed.

then the phone
rang

it was my
girlfriend

she had been calling all
night

she was angry

she accused me of fornicating with
another

I told her about the beautiful
eagles

how they glided

and that I had been with a concrete
man

bullshit
she said
and hung
up

I stretched out there
looked at the ceiling and
wondered what the eagles
ate

then the phone rang
again

and she asked

did the concrete man have a
concrete wife and did you stick you
dick in her?

no
I answered
I fucked an
eagle

she hung up
again

concrete poetry
I thought
what the hell is
it?

then I went to sleep and I
slept and I
slept.

Gay Paree

the cafes in Paris are just like you imagine
they are:
very well-dressed people, snobs, and
the snob-waiter comes up and takes your
order
as if you were a
leper.
but after you get your wine
you feel better
you begin to feel like a snob
yourself
and you give the guy at the next table
a sidelong glance
he catches you and
you twitch your nose
a bit as if you had just smelled
dogshit
then you
look away.

and the food
when it arrives
is always too mild.
the French are delicate with their
spices.

and
as you eat and drink
you realize that everybody is
terrorized:

too bad
too bad

such a lovely city
full of
cowards.

then
more wine brings more
realization:
Paris is the world and the world
is
Paris.

drink to it
and
because of
it.

I thought the stuff tasted worse than usual

I used to drink with Jane
every night
until two or
three
a.m.

and I had to
report for
work
at 5:30
a.m.

one morning
I was sitting
casing mail
next to this
healthy
religious
fellow

and he said,
"hey, I *smell*
something, don't
you?"

I answered in the
negative.

"actually," he said,
"it smells something
like
gasoline."

"well," I told
him, "don't light a
match or
I might
explode."

the blade

there was no parking near the post office where
I worked at night
so I found this splendid spot
(nobody seemed to care to park there)
on a dirt road behind a
slaughterhouse
and as I sat in my car
just before work
smoking a last cigarette
I was treated to the same
scene
as each evening tailed off into
night —
the pigs were herded out of the
yard pens
and onto runways
by a man making pig sounds and
flapping a large canvas
and the pigs ran wildly
up the runway
toward the waiting
blade,
and many evenings
after watching that
after finishing my
smoke
I just started the car
backed out of there and
drove away from my
job.

my absenteeism reached such astonishing
proportions

that I had to finally
park
at some expense
behind a Chinese bar
where all I could see were tiny shuttered
windows
with neon signs advertising some
oriental
libation.

it seemed less real, and that was
what was
needed.

the boil

I was making good with the girls on the assembly line at
Nabisco, I had recently beaten up the company
bully
on my lunch hour,
things were going well, I was from out of
town, the stranger who seldom spoke to
anybody, I was the mystery man, I was the
cool number,
almost all those fillies had an interest
in me
and the guys didn't know
what the hell.

then one morning I awakened in my
room
with a huge boil on the side of
my head (right cheek)
and
it was damn near the size of a
golf ball.

I should have phoned in sick
but
I didn't have the sense and
went on in
anyhow.

it made a difference: the women's eyes
fell away from mine, and the guys
no longer acted fearful
and I felt defeated by
fate.

the boil remained
for
2 days
3 days
4 days.

on the 5th day the foreman handed me
my papers: "we're cutting back, you're
finished."

this was one hour before
lunch.

I walked to my locker, opened it,
took off my apron and cap
threw them in there
along with the
key
and walked
out

a truly horrible walk
to the street
where I turned around
and looked back at the building
feeling as if they had
discovered
something
hideously indecent
about me.

not listed

my horse was the grey
a 4 to one shot
with early lick
and he had a length and
a half
3/4's of the way
down the stretch
when his left front leg
snapped
and he tumbled
tossing the jock
over his neck and
head.
luckily
the field avoided both
the horse and the
jock — who
got up and limped away
from the kicking
animal.

accident potential:
that's something
that's not listed in
the Racing Form.

in the clubhouse
I saw Harry
standing in a far-
off corner.
he was an x-jock's
agent
now working as a

trainer
but not having
too many mounts
to train.

he was behind his
dark shades
looking
awful.

"you have the grey?"
I asked.

"yeah," he said,
"heavy . . ."

"you need a transfusion,
it's not much but . . ."

I slipped
3 folded 20's
into his coat
pocket.

"thanks," he
said.

"put it on a good one."

Harry had done me some
nice things
and anyhow
he was one of the
best
working for an edge
in one of the bloodiest

rackets
around: we are trying to
beat the percentages
and each day
some must fall
so that
others can go
on. (the track is just
like anyplace else
only there
it usually happens
more
quickly.)

I walked over and got
a coffee.
I liked the next
race
a six furlong affair for
non-winners of
two.

one good hit
would put the gods in
place
and cure
everything
in a flash of
glory . . .

I'm not a misogynist

more and more
I get letters from
young ladies:

"I'm a well-built 19
am between jobs and
your writing turns me
on
I'm a good housekeeper
and secretary and
would *never* get in
your way
and
would send a
photo but that's
so tacky . . ."

"I'm 21
tall and attractive
have read your books
I work for a
lawyer and
if you're ever in
town
please call me."

"I met you
after your reading
at the Troubadour
we had a night
together
do you remember?
I married

that man
you told me had a
mean voice
when you phoned and
he answered
we're divorced now
I have a little
girl
age 2
I am no longer in
the music
business but
miss it
would like to
see you
again . . ."

"I've read
all your books
I'm 23
not much
breast
but have *great*
legs
and
just a few
words
from you
would mean
so much
to me . . ."

girls
please give your
bodies and your
lives

to
the young men
who
deserve them

besides
there is
no way
I would welcome
the
intolerable
dull
senseless hell
you would bring
me

and
I wish you
luck
in bed
and
out

but not
in
mine

thank
you.

the lady in the castle

she lived in this house
that looked like a
castle
and when you got inside
the ceilings were so very
high
and I was poor
and it all rather
fascinated
me.

she
was no longer
young
but she had
masses
of hair
that damn near
went down to her
ankles
and
I thought about
how strange
it would be
doing it
with all that
hair.

I drove up there
several times
in my old
car
and she had fine

liquors to
drink
and we sat
but I could
never quite get
near her
and though I didn't
push at
it
something about
not
connecting
did offend my
ego
for ugly as I was
I had always been
lucky with the
ladies.

it confused me
and I suppose
I needed
that.

she liked to
talk about
the arts and
about
film making
and listening
to all that
only made me
drink
more.

I
finally
just
gave her
up
and a good year
or so
went by
when
one night
the phone
rang: it was the
lady.

"I want to come see
you," she said.

"I'm writing now, I'm
hot . . . I can't see
anybody . . ."

"I just want to come
by, I won't bother you,
I'll just sit on the couch,
I'll sleep on the couch, I
won't bother you . . ."

"NO! JESUS CHRIST, I
CAN'T SEE ANYBODY!"

I hung up.

the lady who was *actually*
on the couch
said, "oh, you're all
SOFT now!"

"yeah."

"come here . . ."

she took my penis
in her hand
flicked out her
tongue
then
stopped.

"what are you writing?"

"nothing . . . I've got writer's
block . . ."

"sure you have . . . your pipes are
clogged . . . you need to get
cleaned out . . ."

then she had me in her
mouth

and then the phone rang
again . . .

in a fury
I ran over to the
phone
picked it
up.

it was the lady in the
castle:

"listen, I won't bother you,
you won't even know I'm
there . . ."

"YOU WHORE, I'M GETTING A
BLOW JOB!"

I hung up and
turned back.

the other lady was walking
toward the
door.

"what'sa matter?" I
asked.

"I can't STAND that
term!"

"what term?"

"BLOW JOB!" she
screamed.

she slammed the door and
was gone . . .

I walked to where the
typewriter sat
put a new piece of paper
in there.
it was one
a.m.

I sat there and
drank scotch and
beer chasers
smoked cheap
cigars.

3:15 a.m.
I was still sitting
there
re-lighting old
cigar stubs and
drinking ale.

the new
piece of paper was still
unused.

I switched out the
lights
worked my way toward
the bedroom
got myself on the
bed
clothes still
on

I could hear the toilet
running
but couldn't get up
to tap the handle
to end that
sound

my god damned pipes were
clogged.

relentless as the tarantula

they're not going to let you
sit at a front table
at some cafe in Europe
in the mid-afternoon sun.
if you do, somebody's going to
drive by and
spray your guts with a
submachine gun.

they're not going to let you
feel good
for very long
anywhere.
the forces aren't going to
let you sit around
fucking-off and
relaxing.
you've got to do it
their way.

the unhappy, the bitter and
the vengeful
need their
fix — which is
you or somebody
anybody
in agony, or
better yet
dead, dropped into some
hole.

as long as there are
human beings about

there is never going to be
any peace
for any individual
upon this earth (or
anywhere else
they might
escape to).

all you can do
is maybe grab
ten lucky minutes
here
or maybe an hour
there.

something
is working toward you
right now, and
I mean you
and nobody but
you.

their night

never could read *Tender Is the
Night*
but they've made a
tv adaptation of the
book
and it's been running
for several
nights
and I have spent
ten minutes
here and there
watching the troubles of
the rich
while they are leaning
against their beach chairs
in Nice
or walking about their
large rooms
drink in hand while
making
philosophical
statements
or
fucking up
at the
dinner party
or the
dinner dance
they really have no
idea
of what to do with
themselves:
swim?

tennis?
drive up the
coast?
down the
coast?
find
new beds?
lose old
ones?
or
fuck with the
arts and the
artists?

having nothing to struggle
against
they have nothing to struggle
for.

the rich are different
all right

so is the ring-
tailed
maki and the
sand
flea.

huh?

in
Germany France Italy
I can walk down the streets and be
followed by
young men laughing
young ladies
giggling and
old
ladies turning their noses
up . . .

while
in America
I am just another
tired
old man
doing whatever
tired old men
do.

oh, this has its
compensations:
I can take my pants
to the cleaners or
stand in a
supermarket line
without any
hubbub at
all:
the gods have allowed me
a gentle
anonymity.

yet
at times
I do consider my
overseas fame
and
the only thing
I can come up with is
that
I must have some
great motherfucking
translators.

I must
owe them
the hair on my
balls
or
possibly

my balls

themselves.

it's funny, isn't it? #1

we were standing around
at this birthday party
at this fancy
restaurant

and
many
special people were
about
preening their
fame.

I wanted to run
out

when a man
standing near by
said something
exactly appropriate
to the
occasion.

"hey," I said to
my wife, "this
guy's got
something. when we are
seated
let's try to
sit next to
him."

we did and as
the drinks were

poured
the man began
talking

he began on a
long story
which was
building toward a
punch
line.

my problem was that
I could guess
what the
punch line
was
going to
be.

and
he talked
on and
on

then
dropped the
line.

"shit," I
told him, "that
was
awful, you've
really
disappointed
me . . ."

he
only began
on another
story.

I walked over to
another table
and stood behind
the now
great
movie star.

"listen,
when I first met
you
you were just a nice
German boy.
now
you've turned into
a
conceited
prick. you've
really
disappointed
me."

the great movie
star (who was a
man
mighty of
muscle) growled
and
shook his
shoulders.

then I walked over to
the table
where the birthday lady
sat
surrounded by
all these
media
folk.

"looking at you
people," I said, "makes
me feel like
vomiting
all over
your
inept
plausibilities!"

"oh," said the lady
to her
guests, "he
always talks
that
way!"

and she gave a
laugh, poor
dear.

so
I said, "Happy
birthday,
but
I warned you
never to

invite me to these
things."

then
I walked back to
my table

motioned the waiter
for
another
drink.

the man
was telling
another
story

but
it was not
nearly
as good
as

this
one.

it's funny, isn't it? #2

when we were kids
laying around the lawn
on our
bellies

we often talked
about
how
we'd like to
die

and
we all
agreed on the
same
thing:

we'd all
like to die
fucking

(although
none of us
had
done any
fucking)

and now
that
we are hardly
kids
any longer

we think more
about
how
not to
die

and
although
we're
ready

most of
us
would
prefer to
do it
alone

under the
sheets

now
that

most of
us

have fucked
our lives
away.

the beautiful lady editor

she was a beautiful woman, I used to see photographs of
her in the literary magazines of that
day.

I was young but always alone — I felt that I needed the
time to get something done and the only way I could buy time
was with
poverty.

I worked not so much with craft but more with getting down
what was edging me toward madness — and I had
flashes of luck, but it was hardly a pleasurable
existence.

I think I showed a fine endurance but slowly then
health and courage began to leak away.

and the night arrived when everything fell apart — and
fear, doubt, humiliation entered . . .

and I wrote a number of letters using my last stamps
telling a few select people that I had made a
mistake, that I was starving and trapped in a small
freezing shack of darkness in a strange city in
a strange
state.

I mailed the letters and then I waited long wild days and
nights, hoping, yearning at last for a decent
response.

only two letters ever arrived — on the same day —
and I opened the pages and shook the pages looking for

money but there was
none.

one letter was from my father, a six-pager telling me that
I deserved what was happening, that I should have become
an engineer like he told me, and that nobody would ever read
the kind of stuff I wrote, and on and on, like
that.

the other letter was from the beautiful lady editor, neatly typed
    on
expensive stationery, and she said that she was no longer
publishing her literary magazine, that she had found God and
    was
living in a castle on a hill in Italy and helping the poor, and
she signed her famous name, with a "God Bless you," and that
    was
that.

ah, you have no idea, in that dark freezing shack, how much I
    wanted to
be poor in Italy instead of Atlanta, to be a poor peasant,
yes, or even a dog on her bedspread, or even a flea on that
dog on that
bedspread: how much I wanted the tiniest
warmth.

the lady had published me along with Henry Miller, Sartre,
    Celine,
others.

I should never have asked for money in a world where millions
    of
peasants were crawling the starving
streets

and even some years later when the lady editor
died
I still thought her
beautiful.

about the PEN conference

take a writer away from his typewriter
and all you have left
is
the sickness
which started him
typing
in the
beginning.

everybody talks too much

when
the cop pulled me
over
I
handed him my
license.
he
went back
to radio in
the make
and model
of my car
and
get clearance on
my plates.

he wrote
the ticket
walked
up
handed it
to me
to
sign.

I did
he gave
me
back the
license.

"how come
you

don't
say
anything?"
he asked.

I shrugged
my
shoulders.

"well, sir,"
he
said, "have
a
good day
and
drive
carefully."

I
noticed
some sweat
on his
brow
and the
hand
that held
the
ticket
seemed to
be
trembling
or
perhaps
I
was only
imagining it?

anyhow
I
watched him
move
toward
his
bike
then I
pulled
away . . .

when confronted
with
dutiful
policemen
or
women
in rancor
I
have nothing
to
say
to them

for
if I
truly
began
it would
end
in
somebody's
death:
theirs or
mine

so
I
let them
have
their
little
victories
which
they need
far
more
than
I
do.

me and my buddy

I can still see us
together
back then
sitting by the river
while shit-
faced on the
grape
and playing with the
poem
knowing it to be
utterly useless
but something to
do
while
waiting

the Emperors
with their frightened
clay faces
watch us as we
drink

Li Po crumbles his
poems
sets them on
fire
floats them down the
river.

"what have you
done?" I
ask him.

Li passes the
bottle: "they are
going to end
no matter what
happens . . ."

I drink to his
knowledge
pass the bottle
back

sit tightly upon my
poems
which I have
jammed halfway up my
crotch

I help him burn
some more of his
poesy

they float well
down
the river
lighting up the
night
as good words
should.

song

Julio came by with his guitar and sang his
latest song.
Julio was famous, he wrote songs and also
published books of little drawings and
poems.
they were very
good.

Julio sang a song about his latest love
affair.
he sang that
it began so well
then it went to
hell.

those were not the words exactly
but that was the meaning of the
words.

Julio finished
singing.

then he said, "I still care for
her, I can't get her off my
mind."

"what will I do?" Julio
asked.

"drink," Henry said,
pouring.

Julio just looked at his
glass:
"I wonder what she's doing
now?"

"probably engaging in oral
copulation," Henry
suggested.

Julio put his guitar back in
the case and
walked to the
door.

Henry walked Julio to his car which
was parked in the
drive.

it was a nice moonlit
night.

as Julio started his car and
backed out the drive
Henry waved him a
farewell.

then he went inside
sat
down.

he finished Julio's untouched
drink
then he
phoned
her.

"he was just by," Henry told
her, "he's feeling very
bad . . ."

"you'll have to excuse me,"
she said, "but I'm busy right
now."

she hung
up.

and Henry poured one of his
own
as outside the crickets sang
their own
song.

practice

in that depression neighborhood I had two buddies
Eugene and Frank
and I had wild fist fights with each of
them
once or twice a week.
the fights lasted 3 or 4 hours and we came out
with
smashed noses, fattened lips, black eyes, sprained
wrists, bruised knuckles, purple
welts.

our parents said nothing, let us fight on and
on
watching disinterestedly and
finally going back to their newspapers
or their radios or their thwarted sex lives,
they only became angry if we tore or ruined our
clothing, and for that and only for that.

but Eugene and Frank and I
we had some good work-outs
we rumbled through the evenings, crashing through
hedges, fighting along the asphalt, over the
curbings and into strange front and backyards of
unknown homes, the dogs barking, the people screaming at
us.
we were
maniacal, we never quit until the call for supper
which none of us could afford to
miss.

anyhow, Eugene became a Commander in the

Navy and Frank became a Supreme Court Justice, State of
California and I fiddled with the
poem.

love poem to a stripper

50 years ago I watched the girls
shake it and strip
at The Burbank and The Follies
and it was very sad
and very dramatic
as the light turned from green to
purple to pink
and the music was loud and
vibrant,
now I sit here tonight
smoking and
listening to classical
music
but I still remember some of
their names: Darlene, Candy, Jeanette
and Rosalie.
Rosalie was the
best, she knew how,
and we twisted in our seats and
made sounds
as Rosalie brought magic
to the lonely
so long ago.

now Rosalie
either so very old or
so quiet under the
earth,
this is the pimple-faced
kid
who lied about his
age

just to watch
you.

you were good, Rosalie
in 1935,
good enough to remember
now
when the light is
yellow
and the nights are
slow.

my buddy

for a 21-year-old boy in New Orleans I wasn't worth
much: I had a dark small room that smelled of
piss and death
yet I just wanted to stay in there, and there were
two lively girls down at the end of the hall who
kept knocking on my door and yelling, "Get up!
There are good things out here!"

"Go away," I told them, but that only goaded
them on, they left notes under my door and
scotch-taped flowers to the
doorknob.

I was on cheap wine and green beer and
dementia . . .

I got to know the old guy in the next
room, somehow I felt old like
him; his feet and ankles were swollen and he couldn't
lace his shoes.

each day about one p.m. we went for a walk
together and it was a very slow
walk: each step was painful for
him.

as we came to the curbing I helped him
up and down
gripping him by an elbow
and the back of his
belt, we made it.

I liked him: he never questioned me about
what I was or wasn't
doing.

he should have been my father, and I liked
best what he said over and
over: "Nothing is worth
it."

he was a
sage.

those young girls should have
left him the
notes and the
flowers.

Jon Edgar Webb

I had a lyric poem period down in New Orleans, pounding
out these fat rolling lines and
drinking gallons of beer.
it felt good like screaming in a madhouse, the madhouse of
my world
as the mice scattered among the
empties.
at times I went into the bars
but I couldn't work it out with those people who sat on the
stools:
men evaded me and the women were terrified of
me.
bartenders asked that I
leave.
I did, struggling back with wondrous six-packs
to the room and the mice and those fat rolling
lines.

that lyric poem period was a raving bitch of a
time
and there was an editor right around the
corner who
fed each page into a waiting press, rejecting
nothing
even though I was unknown
he printed me upon ravenous paper
manufactured to last
2,000 years.

this editor who was also the publisher and
the printer
kept a straight face as I handed him the ten to
twenty pages

each morning:
"is that all?"

that crazy son of a bitch, he was a lyric
poem
himself.

thank you

some want me to go on writing about whores
and puking.

others say that type of thing disgusts
them.

well, I don't miss the
whores

although now and then one or another makes an
attempt to locate
me.

I don't know if they miss all the booze and
the bit of money I gave them

or if they are enthralled at the way
I've immortalized them in
literature.

anyhow, they must now make do with
whatever men
they are able to scrounge
up.

— those poor darlings had no
idea . . .

and neither did I
that those ugly roaring nights
would be fodder

such as even
Dostoevski
would not shy away
from.

the magic curse

I never liked skid-row and so I stayed away from the soup
kitchens, the bloodbanks and all the so-called hand-
outs.

I got so god damned thin that if
I turned sidewise it was hard to see my shadow under a
hard noon sun.

it didn't matter to me so long as I stayed away from the
crowd

and even down there it was a
successful and an unsuccessful
crowd.

I don't think I was insane
but many of the
insane think
that

but I think
now
if anything saved me
it was the avoidance of the
crowd

it was my
food

still
is.

get me in a room with more than
3 people
I tend to act
ill
odd.

I once
even asked my wife: look, I must be
sick . . . perhaps I ought to see a
shrink?

Christ, I said, he might cure me
and then what would I
do?

she just looked at me
and we forgot the
whole
thing.

party's over

after you've pulled off the tablecloth with
the full plates of food
and broken the windows
and rung the bells of
idiots
and have
spoken true and terrible
words
and have
chased the mob through the
doorway—
then comes the great and
peaceful moment: sitting alone
and
pouring that quiet drink.

the world is better without
them.

only the plants and the animals are
true comrades.

I drink to them and with
them.

they wait as I fill their
glasses.

no nonsense

Faulkner loved his whiskey
and along with the
writing
he didn't have
time
for much
else.

he didn't open
most of his
mail

just held it up
to the light

and if it didn't
contain a
check

he trashed
it.

escape

the best part was
pulling down the
shades
stuffing the doorbell
with rags
putting the phone
in the
refrigerator
and going to bed
for 3 or 4
days.

and the next best
part
was
nobody ever
missed
me.

wearing the collar

I live with a lady and four cats
and some days we all get
along.

some days I have trouble with
one of the
cats.

other days I have trouble with
two of the
cats.

other days,
three.

some days I have trouble with
all four of the
cats

and the
lady:

ten eyes looking at me
as if I was a dog.

a cat is a cat is a cat is a cat

she's whistling and clapping
for the cats
at 2 a.m.
as I sit in here
with my
Beethoven.

"they're just prowling," I
tell her . . .

Beethoven rattles his bones
majestically

and those damn cats
don't care
about
any of it

and
if they did
I wouldn't like them
as
well:

things begin to lose their
natural value
when they approach
human
endeavor.

nothing against
Beethoven:

he did fine
for what he
was

but I wouldn't want
him
on my rug
with one leg
over his head
while
he was
licking
his balls.

marching through Georgia

we are burning like a chicken wing left on the grill of an
outdoor barbecue
we are unwanted and burning we are burning and unwanted
    we are
an unwanted
burning
as we sizzle and fry
to the bone
the coals of Dante's *Inferno* spit and sputter beneath
us
   and
above the sky is an open hand
   and
the words of wise men are useless
it's not a nice world, a nice world it's
not . . .

come on, try this nice burnt chicken-wing poem
it's hot it's tough not much
meat
but 'tis sadly sensible
and one or two bites ends it
thus

gone

it left like the ladies of old
as I opened the door
to the room
bed
pillows
walls

I lost it
I lost it somewhere
while walking down the street
or while lifting weights
or while watching a parade
I lost it
while watching a wrestling match

or while waiting at a red light
at noon on some smoggy day

I lost it while putting a coin
into a parking meter

I lost it
as the wild dogs slept.

I meet the famous poet

this poet had long been famous
and after some decades of
obscurity I
got lucky
and this poet appeared
interested
and asked me to his
beach apartment.
he was homosexual and I was
straight, and worse, a
lush.

I came by, looked
about and
declaimed (as if I didn't
know), "hey, where the
fuck are the
babes?"

he just smiled and stroked
his mustache.

he had little lettuces and
delicate cheeses and
other dainties
in his refrigerator.
"where you keep your fucking
beer, man?" I
asked.

it didn't matter, I had
brought my own

bottles and I began upon
them.

he began to look
alarmed: "I've heard about
your brutality, please
desist from
that!"

I flopped down on his
couch, belched,
laughed: "ah, shit, baby, I'm
not gonna hurt ya! ha, ha,
ha!"

"you are a fine writer," he
said, "but as a person you are
utterly
despicable!"

"that's what I like about me
best, baby!" I
continued to pour them
down.

at once
he seemed to vanish behind
some sliding wooden
doors.

"hey, baby, come on
out! I ain't gonna do no
bad! we can sit around and
talk that dumb literary
bullshit all night
long! I won't

brutalize you,
shit, I
promise!"

"I don't trust you,"
came the little
voice.

well, there was nothing to
do
but slug it down, I was
too drunk to drive
home.

when I awakened in the
morning he was standing over
me
smiling.

"uh," I said,
"hi . . ."

"did you mean what you
said last night?" he
asked.

"uh, what wuz
ut?"

"I slid the doors back and
stood there and you saw
me and you said that
I looked like I was riding the
prow of some great sea

ship . . . you said that
I looked like a
Norseman! is
that true?"

"oh, yeah, yeah, you
did . . ."

he fixed me some hot tea
with toast
and I got that
down.

"well," I said, "good to
have met
you . . ."

"I'm sure," he
answered.

the door closed behind
me
and I found the elevator
down
and
after some wandering about the
beach front
I found my car, got
in, drove off
on what appeared to be
favorable terms
between the famous poet and
myself

but
it wasn't
so:

he started writing un-
believably hateful stuff
about
me
and I
got my shots in at
him.

the whole matter
was just about
like
most other writers
meeting

and
anyhow
that part about
calling him a
Norseman
wasn't true at
all: I called him
a
Viking

and it also
isn't true
that without his
aid
I never would have
appeared in the
Penguin Collection of
Modern Poets

along with him
and who
was it?

yeah:
Lamantia.

seize the day

foul fellow he was always wiping his nose on his
sleeve and also farting at regular
intervals, he was
uncombed
uncouth
unwanted.
his every third word was a crass
entrail
and he grinned through broken yellow
teeth
his breath stinking above the
wind
he continually dug into his crotch
left-
handed
and he always had a
dirty joke
at the ready,
a dunce of the lowest
order
a most most
avoided
man

until

he won the state
lottery.

now
you should see
him: always a young laughing lady on
each arm

he eats at the finest
places
the waiters fighting to get him
at their
table
he belches and farts away the
night
spilling his wineglass
picking up his steak with his
fingers
while
his ladies call him
"original" and "the funniest
man I ever met."
and what they do to him
in bed
is a damned
shame.

what we have to keep
remembering, though, is that
50% of the state lottery is given to the
Educational System and
that's important
when you realize that
only one person in
nine
can properly spell
"emulously."

the shrinking island

I'm working on it as
the dawn bends toward me . . .

I almost had it at 3:34 a.m. but it
slipped away from me
with the wizardry of a
silverfish . . .

now
as the half-light moves toward me
like motherfucking death
I give up the battle
rise
move toward the bathroom
bang
into a wall
give a pitiful mewking
laugh . . .
flick on the light and
begin to piss, yes, in
the proper place
and
after flushing
think: another night
gone.
well, we gave it a bit of
a roar
anyhow.

we wash our
claws . . .
flick off the
light

move toward the
bedroom where the
wife
awakens enough
to say: "don't step
on the cat!"

which brings us back
to
matters
real
as we find the bed
slip in
face to ceiling: a
grounded
drunken
fat
old
man.

magic machine

I liked the old records that
scratched
as the needle slid across
grooves well
worn
you heard the voice
coming through
the speaker
as if there were a person
inside that
mahogany
box

but you only listened while
your parents were
not there.
and if you didn't wind
the victrola
it gradually slowed and
stopped.

it was best in late
afternoons
and the records spoke
of
love.
love, love, love.
some of the records had
beautiful purple
labels,
others were orange, green,
yellow, red, blue.

the victrola had belonged to
my grandfather
and he had listened to those
same
records.
and now I was a boy
and
I heard them.
and nothing I could think of
in my life then
seemed better than listening
to that
victrola
when my parents weren't
there.

those girls we followed home

in Jr. High the two prettiest girls were
Irene and Louise,
they were sisters;
Irene was a year older, a little taller
but it was difficult to choose between
them;
they were not only pretty but they were
astonishingly beautiful
so beautiful
that the boys stayed away from them;
they were terrified of Irene and
Louise
who weren't aloof at all,
even friendlier than most
but
who seemed to dress a bit
differently than the other
girls:
they always wore high heels,
silk stockings,
blouses,
skirts,
new outfits
each day;
and,
one afternoon
my buddy, Baldy, and I followed them
home from school;
you see, we were kind of
the bad guys on the grounds
so it was
more or less
expected,

and
it was something:
walking along ten or twelve feet behind them;
we didn't say anything
we just followed
watching
their voluptuous swaying,
the balancing of the
haunches.

we liked it so much that we
followed them home from school
every
day.

when they'd go into their house
we'd stand outside on the sidewalk
smoking cigarettes and talking.

"someday," I told Baldy,
"they are going to invite us inside their
house and they are going to
fuck us."

"you really think so?"

"sure."

now
50 years later
I can tell you
they never did
—never mind all the stories we
told the guys;
yes, it's the dream that

keeps you going
then and
now.

fractional note

the flowers are burning
the rocks are melting
the door is stuck inside my head
it's one hundred and two degrees in Hollywood
and the messenger stumbles
dropping the last message into a
hole in the earth
400 miles deep.
the movies are worse than ever
and the dead books of dead men read dead.
the white rats run the treadmill.
the bars stink in swampland darkness
as the lonely unfulfill the lonely.

there's no clarity.
there was never meant to be clarity.

the sun is diminishing, they say.
wait and see.

gravy barks like a dog.

if I had a grandmother
my grandmother could whip your
grandmother.

free fall.
free dirt.
shit costs money.
check the ads for sales . . .

now everybody is singing at once
terrible voices

coming from torn throats.
hours of practice.

it's almost entirely waste.
regret is *mostly* caused by not having
done anything.
the mind barks like a dog.
pass the gravy.

it is so arranged all the way to
oblivion.
next meter reading date:
JUN 20.

and I feel good.

a following

the phone rang at 1:30 a.m.
and it was a man from Denver:

"Chinaski, you got a following in
Denver . . ."

"yeah?"

"yeah, I got a magazine and I want some
poems from you . . ."

"FUCK YOU, CHINASKI!" I heard a voice
in the background . . .

"I see you have a friend,"
I said.

"yeah," he answered, "now, I want
six poems . . ."

"CHINASKI SUCKS! CHINASKI'S A PRICK!"
I heard the other
voice.

"you fellows been drinking?"
I asked.

"so what?" he answered. "you drink."

"that's true . . ."

"CHINASKI'S AN ASSHOLE!"

then
the editor of the magazine gave me the
address and I copied it down on the back
of an envelope.

"send us some poems now . . ."

"I'll see what I can do . . ."

"CHINASKI WRITES SHIT!"

"goodbye," I said.

"goodbye," said the
editor.

I hung up.

there are certainly any number of lonely
people without much to do with
their nights.

a tragic meeting

I was more visible and available then
and I had this great weakness:
I thought that going to bed with many women
meant that a man was clever and good and
superior
especially if he did it at the age of
55
to any number of bunnies
and I lifted weights
drank like mad
and did
that.

most of the women were nice
and most of them looked good
and only one or two were really dumb and
dull
but JoJo
I can't even categorize.
her letters were slight, repeated
the same things:
"I like your books, would like to meet
you . . ."
I wrote back and told her
it would be
all right.

then along came the instructions
where I was to meet
her: at this college
on this date
at this time

just after her
classes.

the college was up in the
hills and
the day and time
arrived
and with her drawings
of twisting streets
plus a road map
I set out.

it was somewhere between the Rose Bowl
and one of the largest graveyards in
Southern California
and I got there early and sat in my
car
nipping at the Cutty Sark
and looking at the
co-eds — there were so many of
them, one simply couldn't have
them *all.*

then the bell rang and I got out of my
car and walked to the front of the
building, there was a long row of
steps and the students walked out of the
building and down the steps
and I stood and
waited, and like with airport
arrivals
I had no idea
which one
it would be.

"Chinaski," somebody said
and there she was: 18, 19,
neither ugly nor beautiful, of
average body and features,
seeming to be neither vicious,
intelligent, dumb or
insane.

we kissed lightly and then
I asked her if she
had a car
and she said
she had a car
and I said, "fine, I'll drive you
to it, then you follow
me . . ."

JoJo was a good follower, she followed me all
the way to my beat-up court in east
Hollywood.

I poured her a drink and we talked very
drab talk and kissed a
bit.
the kisses were neither good nor bad
nor interesting or un-
interesting.

much time went by and she drank very
little
and we kissed some more and she said,
"I like your books, they really do things
to me."
"Fuck my books!" I told her.
I was down to my shorts and I had her
skirt up to her ass

and I was working hard
but she just kissed and
talked.
she responded and she didn't
respond.

then
I gave up and started drinking
heavily.
she mentioned a few of the other
writers
she liked
but she didn't like any of them
the way she liked
me.

"yeah," I poured a new one, "is that
so?"

"I've got to get going," JoJo said,
"I've got a class in the
morning."

"you can sleep here," I suggested, "and
get an early start, I scramble great
eggs."

"no, thank you, I've got to
go . . ."

and she left with
several copies of my books
she had never seen
before,
copies I had given her

much *earlier* in the
evening.

I had another drink and decided to
sleep it off
as an unexplainable
loss.

I switched off the lights
and threw myself upon the
bed without
washing-up or
brushing my
teeth.

I looked up into the dark
and thought, now, here is one
I will never be able to
write about:
she was neither good nor bad,
real or unreal, kind or
unkind, she was just a girl
from a college
somewhere between the Rose Bowl and
the dumping grounds.

then I began to itch, I scratched
myself, I seemed to feel things
on my face, on my belly, I inhaled,
exhaled, tried to sleep but
the itching got worse, then
I felt a bite, then several bites,
things appeared to be
crawling on me . . .

I rushed to the bathroom
and switched on the light

my god, JoJo had *fleas*.

I stepped into the shower
stood there
adjusting the water,
thinking,
that poor
dear
girl.

an ordinary poem

since you've always wanted
to know I am going to admit that I never liked Shakespeare,
    Browning, the
Bronte sisters,
Tolstoy, baseball, summers on the shore, arm-
wrestling, hockey, Thomas Mann, Vivaldi, Winston Churchill,
    Dudley
Moore, free verse,
pizza, bowling, the Olympic Games, the Three Stooges, the
    Marx
Brothers, Ives, Al Jolson, Bob Hope, Frank Sinatra, Mickey
Mouse, basketball,
fathers, mothers, cousins, wives, shack jobs (although preferable
to the former),
and I don't like the Nutcracker Suite, the Academy Awards,
    Hawthorne,
Melville, pumpkin pie, New Year's Eve, Christmas, Labor Day,
    the
Fourth of July, Thanksgiving, Good Friday, The Who,
Bacon, Dr. Spock, Blackstone and Berlioz, Franz
Liszt, pantyhose,
lice, fleas, goldfish, crabs, spiders, war
heroes, space flights, camels (I don't trust camels) or the
Bible,
Updike, Erica Jong, Corso, bartenders, fruit flies, Jane
Fonda,
churches, weddings, birthdays, newscasts, watch
dogs, .22 rifles, Henry
Fonda
and all the women who should have loved me but
didn't and
the first day of Spring and the
last

and the first line of this poem
and this one
that you're reading
now.

from an old dog in his cups . . .

ah, my friend, it's awful, worse
than that—you just get
going good—
one bottle down and
gone—
the poems simmering in your
head
but
halfway between 60 and
70
you pause
before opening the
second bottle—
sometimes
don't
for after 50 years of
heavy drinking
you might assume
that extra bottle
will set you
babbling in some
rest home
or tender you
a stroke
alone in your
place
the cats chewing at
your flesh
as the morning fog
enters the broken
screen.

one doesn't even *think* of
the liver
and if the liver
doesn't think of
us, that's
fine.

but it does seem
the more we drink
the better the words
go.

death doesn't matter
but the ultimate inconvenience
of near-death is worse than
galling.

I'll finish the night off
with
beer.

let 'em go

let's let the bombs go
I'm tired of waiting

I've put away my toys
folded the road maps
canceled my subscription to *Time*
kissed Disneyland goodbye

I've taken the flea collars off my cats
unplugged the tv
I no longer dream of pink flamingoes
I no longer check the market index

let's let 'em go
let's let 'em blow

I'm tired of waiting

I don't like this kind of blackmail
I don't like governments playing cutesy with my life:
either crap or get off the pot
I'm tired of waiting
I'm tired of dangling
I'm tired of the fix

let the bombs blow

you cheap sniveling cowardly nations
you mindless giants

do it
do it
do it!

and escape to your planets and space stations
then you can fuck it
up there too.

trying to make it

new jock in from Arizona
doesn't know this town
but his agent did get him a mount
in the first race
last Saturday
and the jock took the freeway
in
on the same day as
the U.S.C. vs. U.C.L.A. football
game
and got caught
in one of the two special lanes
which took him to the Rose Bowl
instead of the race
track.
he was forced to drive all the way
to the football game
parking lot
before he could turn
around.
by the time he got to the track
the first race
was over.
another jock had won with his
mount.

today out there
I noticed on the program that the
new jock from Arizona
had a good mount in the
6th.
then the horse became a late
scratch.

sometimes getting started
in the big time
is tantamount to
trying to raise an erection
in a tornado
and even if you do
nobody has the time
to notice.

the death of a splendid neighborhood

there was a place off Western Ave.
where you went up a stairway
to get head
and there was a big biker
sitting there
wearing his swastika jacket.
he was there to smell you out
if you were the
heat
and to protect the girls
if you weren't.
it was just above the
Philadelphia Hoagie Shop
there in L.A.
where the girls came down
when things got
slow
and ate something
else.
the man who ran the
sandwich shop
hated the girls
he didn't like to
serve them
but he was
afraid not
to.

then one day
I came by
and the biker wasn't there
or the girls
either,

and it hadn't been a simple
bust
it had been a
shoot-out:
there were bullet holes
in the door
above the
stairway.

I went into the Hoagie shop
for a sandwich and a
beer
and the proprietor told
me,
"things are better
now."

after that
I had to leave town
for a couple of
days
and when I got back
and walked down
to the Hoagie shop
I saw that the plate glass
window
had been busted
out
and was covered with
boards.
inside the walls
and the counter had been
blackened by
fire.

about that same
time
my girlfriend went crazy
and started screwing one man
after
another.

almost everything good was
gone.
I gave my landlord a month's
notice and moved in
3 weeks.

you get so alone at times that it just makes sense

when I was a starving writer I used to read the major writers
    in the
major magazines (in the library, of course) and it made me feel
very bad because—being a student of the word and the way, I
    realized
that they were faking it: I could sense each false emotion, each
utter pretense, it made me feel that the editors had their
heads up their asses—or were being politicized into publishing
in-groups of power
but
I just kept writing and not eating very much—went down
    from 197 pounds
to 137—but—got very much practice typing and reading
    printed rejection
slips.

it was when I reached 137 pounds that I said, to hell with it,
    quit
typing and concentrated on drinking and the streets and the
    ladies of
the streets—at least those people didn't read *Harper's, The
    Atlantic* or
Poetry, a magazine of verse.

and frankly, it was a fair and refreshing ten year lay-off

then I came back and tried it again to find that the editors still
    had
their heads up their asses and/or etc.
but I was up to 225 pounds

rested
and full of background music—

ready to give it another shot in the
dark.

a good gang, after all

I keep hearing from the old dogs,
men who have been writing for
decades,
poets all,
they're still at their
typers
writing better than
ever
past wives and wars and
jobs
and all the things that
happen.
many I disliked for personal
and artistic
reasons . . .
but what I overlooked was
their endurance and
their ability to
improve.

these old dogs
living in smoky rooms
pouring the
bottle . . .

they lash against the
typer ribbons: they came
to
fight.

this

being drunk at the typer beats being with any woman
I've ever seen or known or heard about
like
Joan of Arc, Cleopatra, Garbo, Harlow, M.M. or
any of the thousands that come and go on that
celluloid screen
or the temporary girls I've seen so lovely
on park benches, on buses, at dances and parties, at
beauty contests, cafes, circuses, parades, department
stores, skeet shoots, balloon flys, auto races, rodeos,
bull fights, mud wrestling, roller derbies, pie bakes,
churches, volleyball games, boat races, county fairs,
rock concerts, jails, laundromats or wherever

being drunk at this typer beats being with any woman
I've ever seen or
known.

hot

there's fire in the fingers and there's fire in the shoes and there's
fire in walking across a room
there's fire in the cat's eyes and there's fire in the cat's
balls
and the wrist watch crawls like a snake across the back of the
dresser
and the refrigerator contains 9,000 frozen red hot dreams
and as I listen to the symphonies of dead composers
I am consumed with a glad sadness
there's fire in the walls
and the snails in the garden only want love
and there's fire in the crabgrass
we are burning burning burning
there's fire in a glass of water
the tombs of India smile like smitten motherfuckers
the meter maids cry alone at one a.m. on rainy nights
there's fire in the cracks of the sidewalks
and
all during the night as I have been drinking and typing these
eleven or twelve poems
the lights have gone off and on
there is a wild wind outside
and in between times
I have sat in the dark here
electric (haha) typer off lights out radio off
drinking in the dark
lighting cigarettes in the dark
there was fire off the match
we are all burning together
burning brothers and sisters
I like it I like it I like
it.

late late
late
poem

you think about the time in
Malibu
after taking the tall girl
to dinner and drinks
you came out to the Volks
and the clutch was
gone
(no Auto Club card)
nothing out there but the
ocean and
25 miles to your
room
(her suitcase there
after an air trip from somewhere
in Texas)
and you say to her, "well,
maybe we'll swim back in," and
she forgets to
smile.

and the problem with
writing these poems
as you get into number 7 or
8 or 9
into the second bottle near
3 a.m.
trying to light your
cigarette with a book of
stamps
after already setting the
wastebasket on fire

once
is
that there is still some
adventure and joy
in typing
as the radio roars its
classical music
but the content
begins to get
thin.

3 a.m. games:

the worst thing is
being drunk

all the lighters gone
dumb

matchbooks
empty

cigarette and cigar stubs
all about

you find a small pack of
matches
with 3 paper
matches

but the matches go
limp against the worn match
cover

shit:
drink without smoke is like
cock without
pussy

you drink some
more
search about

find one paper match of
happiness
carefully scratch it

against the least-worn
empty match
pack

it *flares*!
you've got your
smoke!

you light
up

you flick the match
toward a
tray

it misses

and
like that . . .

a flame rises

everything is BURNING
at last!

: an American Express customer
receipt

: some of the empty match
books

: even one of the dead
lighters

the flame whirls and
leaps

then the whole ashtray of
cigarette and cigar stubs
begins to smoke
as if mouths were inhaling
them

you battle the flames with
various and sundry objects
including your
hands

until finally the flame is
gone and there is nothing but
smoke

as again you get that
re-occurring thought: *I must be
crazy.*

you hear your wife's
voice:

"Hank, are you all
right?"

she's on the other side of
the wall in the
bedroom

"oh, I'm fine . . ."

"I smell smoke . . . is the house burning
down?"

"just a small fire, Linda . . . I got
it . . . go to sleep . . ."

she is the one who got you
the steel wastebasket
after a similar
occurrence

soon she is asleep
again

and you're searching

for more
matches.

someday I'm going to write a primer for crippled saints but meanwhile . . .

as the Bomb sits out there in the hands of a
diminishing species
all you want
is me sitting next to you
with popcorn and Dr. Pepper
as those dull celluloid teeth
chew away at
my remains.

I don't worry too much about the
Bomb—the madhouses are full
enough
and I always remember
after one of the best pieces of ass
I ever had
I went to the bathroom and
masturbated—hard to kill a man
like that with a
Bomb?

anyhow, I've finally shaken
R. Jeffers and Celine from my
belltower
and I sit there alone
with you and
Dostoevsky
as the real and the
artificial heart
continues to
falter,
famished . . .

I love you but
don't know what to
do.

help wanted

I was a crazed young man and then found this book written
    by a
crazed older man and I felt better because he was
able to write it down
and then I found a later book by this same crazed older
man
only to me
he seemed no longer crazed he just appeared to be
dull—
we all hold up well for a while, then inherent with flaws and
skips and misses
most of us
so often deteriorate overnight
into a state so near defecation
that the end result is almost unbearable to the
senses.

luckily, I found a few other crazed men who almost remained
    that
way until they
died.

that's more sporting, you know, and lends a bit more to our
lives
as we attend to our—
inumbrate—
tasks.

sticks and stones . . .

complaint is often the result of an insufficient
ability
to live within
the obvious restrictions of this
god damned cage.
complaint is a common deficiency
more prevalent than
hemorrhoids
and as these lady writers hurl their spiked shoes
at me
wailing that
their poems will never be
promulgated
all that I can say to them
is
show me more leg
show me more ass —
that's all you (or I) have
while
it lasts

and for this common and obvious truth
they screech at me:
MOTHERFUCKER SEXIST PIG!

as if that would stop the way fruit trees
drop their fruit
or the ocean brings in the coni and
the dead spores of the Grecian
Empire

but I feel no grief for being called something
which

I am not;
in fact, it's enthralling, somehow, like a good
back rub
on a frozen night
behind the ski lift at
Aspen.

working

ah, those days when I
ran them
in and out of my
shabby apartment.

god, I was a hairy
ugly
thing

and I backed them
all onto the
springs

flailing
away

I was the mindless
drunken ape
in a sad and
dying
neighborhood.

but strangest
of all
were the
new and continuous
arrivals:

it was a
female
parade

and
I exulted
pranced and
pounced

with hardly
an idea
of what
it
meant.

it was a well-
remembered bed-
room
painted a strange
blue.

and
most of the
ladies
left just before
noon

about the time
the mailman
arrived.

he spoke to me
one day, "my god,
man, where do you
get them all?"

"I don't know," I
told him.

"pardon me," he went
on, "but you don't
exactly look like
God's gift to
women, how do you
do it?"

"I don't know,"
I said.

and it was
true: it just
happened and I
did it

in my blue
bedroom
with my
dead mother's
best lace table
linen
tacked up
over the
window.

I was a
fucking
fool.

over done

he had somehow located me again—he was on the
      telephone—talking
about the old days—
wonder whatever happened to Michael or Ken or
Julie Anne?—
and remember . . . ?

—then
there were his present problems—

—he was a talker—he had always been a
talker—

and I had been a
listener

I had listened because I hadn't wanted to
hurt him
by telling him to shut up
like the others
did
in the old
days

now
he was back

and
I held the phone out
at arm's length
and could still hear the
sound—

I handed the phone to my girlfriend and
she listened for a
while—

finally
I took the phone and told him—

hey, man, we've got to stop, the meat's burning
in the oven!

he said, o.k., man, I'll call you
back—

(one thing I remembered about my
old buddy: he was good for his
word)

I put the phone back on the
receiver—

—we don't have any meat in the
oven, said my
girlfriend—

—yes, we do, I told her,
it's
me.

our laughter is muted by their agony

as the child crosses the street as deep sea divers
dive as the painters paint—
the good fight against terrible odds is the vin-
dication and the glory as the swallow rises toward
the moon—
it is so dark now with the sadness of
people
they were tricked, they were taught to expect the
ultimate when nothing is
promised
now young girls weep alone in small rooms
old men angrily swing their canes at
visions as
ladies comb their hair as
ants search for survival
history surrounds us
and our lives
slink away
in
shame.

murder

competition, greed, desire for fame—
after great beginnings they mostly
write when they don't want to write, they write to
order, they write for Cadillacs and younger
girls—and to pay off
old wives.

they appear on talk shows, attend parties
with their peers.
most go to Hollywood, they become snipers and
gossips
and have more and more affairs with younger
and younger girls and/or
men.
they write between Hollywood and the parties,
it's timeclock writing
and in between the panties and/or the
jockstraps
and the cocaine
many of them manage to screw up with the
IRS.

between old wives, new wives, newer and
newer girls (and/or)
all their royalties and residuals—
the hundreds of thousands of
dollars—
are now suddenly
debts.

the writing becomes a useless
spasm
a jerk-off of a once

mighty
gift.

it happens and happens and
continues to:
the mutilation of talent
the gods seldom
give
but so quickly
take.

what am I doing?

got to stop battling these wild speed jocks on the freeway as
    we
roar through hairline openings with stereo blasting through
noon and evening and darkness
when actually all we want is to sit in cool green gardens
talking quietly over drinks.
what makes us this way?—ingrown toenails?—or that the ladies
are not enough?—what foolishness makes us tweak the nose of
Death
       continually?
are we afraid of the slow bedpan?—or slobbering over half-
cooked peas brought to us by a bored nurse with thick
dumb legs?
what wanton hare-brained impulse makes us floor it with
only one hand on the wheel?
don't we realize the peace of aging
gently?
what hell-call is this to war?

we are the sickest of the breed—as fine museums—great art—
generations of knowledge—are all forgotten
as we find profundity in being an
asshole—
we are going to end up as a
photograph—almost life-sized—hanging
as a warning on the
Traffic Court wall

and people will shudder just a bit and
look the other way

knowing that
too much ego is not
enough.

nervous people

you go in for an item—take it to the clerk at the register—he
doesn't know the price—begs leave—returns after a long
time—stares at the electronic cash register—rings up the
sale with some difficulty: $47,583.64—you don't have it
with you—he laughs—calls for help—another clerk
arrives—after another long time he finds a new total:
$1.27. I pay—then must ask for a bag—I thank the
clerk—walk to parking with the lady I am with—"you
make people nervous," she tells me—

we drive home with the item—we put the item to its task—it
doesn't work—the item has a factory
defect—
"I'll take it back," she says—

I go to the bathroom and piss squarely in the center of the
pot—warfare is just one of the problems which besets everyone
during the life of a decent day.

working out

Van Gogh cut off his ear
gave it to a
prostitute
who flung it away in
extreme
disgust.

Van, whores don't want
ears
they want
money.

I guess that's why you were
such a great
painter: you
didn't understand
much
else.

how is your heart?

during my worst times
on the park benches
in the jails
or living with
whores
I always had this certain
contentment—
I wouldn't call it
happiness—
it was more of an inner
balance
that settled for
whatever was occurring
and it helped in the
factories
and when relationships
went wrong
with the
girls.

it helped
through the
wars and the
hangovers
the backalley fights
the
hospitals.

to awaken in a cheap room
in a strange city and
pull up the shade—
this was the craziest kind of
contentment

and to walk across the floor
to an old dresser with a
cracked mirror —
see myself, ugly,
grinning at it all.

what matters most is
how well you
walk through the
fire.

forget it

now, listen, when I die I don't want any crying, just get the
disposal under way, I've had a full some life, and
if anybody has had an edge, I've
had it, I've lived 7 or 8 lives in one, enough for
anybody.
we are all, finally, the same, so no speeches, please,
unless you want to say he played the horses and was very
good at that.

you're next and I already know something you don't,
maybe.

quiet

sitting tonight
at this
table
by the
window

the woman is
glooming
in the
bedroom

these are her
especially bad
days.

well, I have
mine

so
in deference
to her

the typewriter
is
still.

it's odd,
printing this stuff
by
hand

reminds me of
days

past
when things were
not
going well
in another
fashion.

now
the cat comes to
see
me

he flops
under the table
between my
feet

we are both
melting
in the same
fire.

and, dear
cat, we're still
working with the
poem

and some have
noted
that there's some
"slippage"
here.

well, at age
65, I can
"slip"

plenty, yet still
run rings
around
those pamby
critics.

Li Po knew
what to do:
drink another
bottle and
face
the consequences.

I turn to my
right, see this huge
head (reflected in the
window) sucking at
a cigarette
and

we grin at
each
other.

then
I turn
back

sit here
and
print more words upon this
paper

there is never
a final

grand
statement

and that's the
fix
and the trick
that works
against
us

but
I wish you could see
my
cat

he has a
splash
of white on his
face
against an
orange-yellow
background

and then
as I look up
and into the
kitchen

I see a bright
portion
under the overhead
light

that shades into
darkness

and then into darker
darkness and
I can't see
beyond
that.

it's ours

there is always that space there
just before they get to us
that space
that fine relaxer
the breather
while say
flopping on a bed
thinking of nothing
or say
pouring a glass of water from the
spigot
while entranced by
nothing

that
gentle pure
space

it's worth

centuries of
existence

say

just to scratch your neck
while looking out the window at
a bare branch

that space
there
before they get to us

ensures
that
when they do
they won't
get it all

ever.

CHARLES BUKOWSKI is one of America's best-known contemporary writers of poetry and prose, and, many would claim, its most influential and imitated poet. He was born in Andernach, Germany, to an American soldier father and a German mother in 1920, and brought to the United States at the age of three. He was raised in Los Angeles and lived there for fifty years. He published his first story in 1944 when he was twenty-four and began writing poetry at the age of thirty-five. He died in San Pedro, California, on March 9, 1994, at the age of seventy-three, shortly after completing his last novel, *Pulp* (1994).

During his lifetime he published more than forty-five books of poetry and prose, including the novels *Post Office* (1971), *Factotum* (1975), *Women* (1978), *Ham on Rye* (1982), and *Hollywood* (1989). Among his most recent books are the posthumous editions of *What Matters Most Is How Well You Walk Through the Fire* (1999), *Open All Night: New Poems* (2000), *Beerspit Night and Cursing: The Correspondence of Charles Bukowski and Sheri Martinelli, 1960–1967* (2001), and *The Night Torn Mad with Footsteps: New Poems* (2001).

All of his books have now been published in translation in over a dozen languages and his worldwide popularity remains undiminished. In the years to come, Ecco will publish additional volumes of previously uncollected poetry and letters.

THESE AND OTHER TITLES BY CHARLES BUKOWSKI ARE AVAILABLE FROM

ecco *An Imprint of HarperCollinsPublishers*

ISBN 0-06-057705-3 (hc)
ISBN 0-06-057706-1 (pb)

ISBN 0-06-057703-7 (hc)
ISBN 0-06-057704-5 (pb)

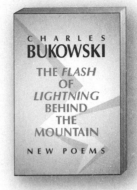

ISBN 0-06-057701-0 (hc)
ISBN 0-06-057702-9 (pb)

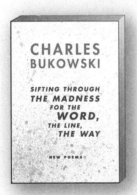

ISBN 0-06-052735-8 (hc)
ISBN 0-06-056823-2 (pb)

ISBN 0-876-85557-5 (pb)

ISBN 0-876-85362-9 (pb)

ISBN 0-876-85086-7 (pb)

ISBN 0-876-85926-0 (pb)

ISBN 0-876-85390-4 (pb)